Dear Reader:

Welcome to my world of L.A. CONNECTIONS. I have been toying with the idea for some time of writing a serial novel, and last year when I wrote a special four-part series for *TV Guide,* and received so many of your wonderful letters, I knew that I wanted to make it bigger and better! L.A. CONNECTIONS is a story about a high-profile murder in Los Angeles. This four-part novel brings together a group of diverse characters—true-life people, cleverly disguised, that I have observed in all the years I have lived in Hollywood.

I know many of you loved the character of Lucky Santangelo, a heroine I created in four of my books: *Chances, Lucky, Lady Boss,* and *Vendetta: Lucky's Revenge.* In L.A. CONNECTIONS, I have tried to create characters just as charismatic.

Writing is my passion, and bringing a serial novel to life is a wonderful challenge. First comes *Power,* followed by *Obsession,* then *Murder,* and finally, *Revenge.*

When you read something that really grabs your attention, it should be a great visual trip so that you can imagine the characters. In all my seventeen books, I feel I've captured the essence of the lives I have observed. Of course, I've changed the names to protect the not-so-innocent!

Writing L.A. CONNECTIONS was an adventure. I hope you join me for all four parts, and that it will keep you reading way into the night.

Stay with me—I promise you we'll have fun!

Happy Reading,

Meet the Men and Women Caught Up in the Danger and the Deception of *MURDER*

Madison Castelli: The feisty, smart, sensual journalist is sent to L.A. to interview Hollywood superagent Freddie Leon for the magazine *Manhattan Style*. Instead she's swept into the biggest crime story of the year, and into a desire that may shatter her tough professionalism or her heart. . . .

Kristin Carr: More Norma Jean than Marilyn, her wholesome, nubile looks are a titillating contrast with her talents—as a high-priced call girl, specializing in rich and famous clients. Risk is all part of her job, and so is servicing Max Steele *and* Mister X.

Freddie Leon: A driven, devious deal-maker who manipulates his celebrity clients like a puppet master, he has enormous power, a hidden agenda, and a star's erotic eight-by-ten glossies locked up in his safe . . . for insurance.

Max Steele: Still boyish looking at 42, in shape, and happiest behind the wheel of a shiny red Maserati or luring a lady into his bedroom, he's Freddie Leon's longtime partner . . . and the worst mistake he could make would be to become his enemy.

Jake Sica: Easy charm, laughing eyes, and sexual heat on sizzle, this freelance photographer holds a natural attraction for any SWF . . . but he has fallen hard, fast, and furiously for a blond beauty whose secrets mask a deadly double life.

Natalie DeBarge: Like a five-foot-two case of dynamite, this black and beautiful, vivacious newscaster just needs some heat to ignite an explosive career. Now with her best friend Madison visiting, she's about to be cast into the fire of a breaking story. . . .

Cole DeBarge: Natalie's handsome, gay brother—a fitness trainer who *really* knows the secrets of the stars.

Mister X: The identity of the man who likes his sex strange, kinky, and dangerous is as hidden as his dark soul. His obsession is to experience ecstasy beyond the limits, where fear and death meet. . . .

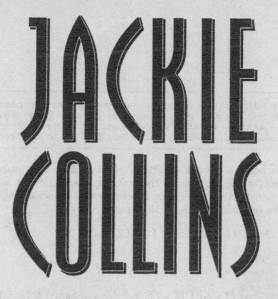

JACKIE COLLINS

Murder

POCKET BOOKS

New York   London   Toronto   Sydney   Tokyo   Singapore

This book is a work of fiction. Names, characters, places and incidents are products of the author's imagination or are used fictitiously. Any resemblance to actual events or locales or persons, living or dead, is entirely coincidental.

An *Original* Publication of POCKET BOOKS

POCKET BOOKS, a division of Simon & Schuster Inc.
1230 Avenue of the Americas, New York, NY 10020

Copyright © 1998 by Chances, Inc.

ISBN: 0-671-02460-4

First Pocket Books printing November 1998

10 9 8 7 6 5 4 3 2 1

POCKET and colophon are registered trademarks of Simon & Schuster Inc.

Back cover photo by Greg Gorman

Printed in the U.S.A.

Murder

chapter 1

The media were in a frenzy. A beautiful blond sex symbol, Salli T. Turner, star of TV's *Teach!*, had been murdered, and the circus was in full swing. Her luxurious mansion in Pacific Palisades was surrounded on all sides by TV trucks, their crews, reporters, and the general populace held back behind police lines.

The slaying of Salli and her houseman, Froo, was already as high profile as the Nicole Simpson/Ron Goldman killings. The media liked nothing better than a good, juicy, violent murder to hang onto, and Salli T. Turner was the perfect victim. A blond goddess, she was known on every continent as the girl in the black rubber swimsuit, thanks to the worldwide success of her TV show and her many photo spreads in numerous popular magazines—including three *Playboy* covers.

Salli had been married twice. Her current husband was Bobby Skorch, a man whose profession was performing dangerous stunts. When Bobby had returned home from Vegas at three A.M., Tucci had confronted him with the shocking news. Bobby had appeared to be so distraught that he'd locked himself in the master bedroom and refused to come out.

Salli's former husband, Eddie Stoner, a small-time actor, was currently under arrest for parking violations. The arrest, however, was a scam—the police had wanted to get him into custody so they could question him, and thirty-four unpaid tickets had seemed a good way to accomplish it.

Detective Chuck Tucci was in charge of the case. A well-built, nice-looking man in his late forties, he'd had two hours of sleep the previous night and was now feeling the effects. He was also aware that very shortly he'd have to give some kind of press conference to satisfy the hordes of media who hovered outside the murdered star's home like hungry vultures waiting for something to be thrown into their gaping mouths. Detective Tucci knew exactly what he'd like to throw—several hand grenades.

Early in the morning his understanding wife, Faye, had packed him a care package—one corned beef, lettuce and tomato sandwich, his favorite, *and* a carton of her homemade coleslaw, which she knew he loved. He'd missed dinner the night before, and when he'd finally arrived home at some ungodly hour, Faye had been asleep. As soon as he'd made enough noise to wake her, though, she got up, and in spite of the fact that he was supposed to be on a diet, she'd hurried down to the kitchen and fixed him a delicious plate of scrambled eggs. Faye was a good woman, also a most attractive one; feisty, with hispanic blood, she was a pocket-sized Venus, with a mass of black hair and kind brown eyes. Detective Tucci often gave thanks for the day he met her: he'd been investigating a murder in Malibu, and she had been the social worker sent to collect the two children in the house. Three months later they were married.

Last night he'd wolfed down the plate of eggs she'd fixed him and begged for more. "You can't eat anything else this late," Faye had scolded, wagging a disapproving finger at him. "It's bad for your stomach."

Bad for his *stomach?* Given half the chance, he would've devoured everything in sight, in spite of the fact that he'd spent the evening in the company of two dead bodies—Salli T. Turner, hacked to death by her frenzied killer, and Froo, her house-man, shot in the face—two bloodied bodies he'd had to inspect and watch being photographed. Finally, when forensics were finished, he'd observed as the bodies were hauled off to be autopsied, and then he prowled around the house, making copious notes in his worn blue leather notebook. After that he interviewed the neighbors, and now, in the morning sunshine, all that was left were the chalk marks to show exactly where the unfortunate victims had fallen.

Detective Tucci shook his head and tried not to think about food. His care package was sitting in the kitchen where he had left it, and there it would stay until he got desperate. He was now waiting to interview the infamous Bobby Skorch. A few hours ago, Bobby's lawyer, Marty Steiner, arrived at the house and rushed straight to the bedroom, where he'd been huddled with his client for the last two hours. Marty was smoothness personified, with his slicked-back silver hair, smug face and expensive jogging suit. A "dream team" reject, he was a man obviously determined to hit the headlines. One look and Tucci had immediately tagged him "Hollywood lawyer," although he'd promised himself not to make such quick judgments. Faced with Marty Steiner, the temptation proved irresistible.

He glanced at his watch, noting that the brown leather strap was worn and that he needed to buy a new one. Maybe next weekend he and Faye would go shopping. Faye loved wandering along the Third Street promenade, checking out the stores, and as long as they got to stop for a hamburger or a hot dog, he didn't object.

Now that his mind was back on food, his sandwich, tightly packaged in Saran Wrap, sitting quietly in the kitchen, was beckoning him. Finally he gave up and hurried into the kitchen.

Salli T. Turner's plump, middle-aged Filipino maid, Eppie, sat at the end of a long marble counter, crying into a glass of milk and a plate full of cookies. Earlier he had questioned her; between sobs she told him she didn't know anything. According to Eppie, she arrived at the house every morning at eight A.M. and departed at three P.M. When she left yesterday, Missy Salli—as she called her employer—had been happily having lunch out by the pool. He'd asked her about Bobby Skorch. "They very much in love," Eppie had answered tearily. "Always laughing."

Well Bobby Skorch wasn't laughing now, Tucci thought grimly. And he wasn't talking either. Not that he had any obligation to do so—but if he didn't, it would cast a deep pall of suspicion over him.

Tucci's eyes swiveled to the end of the marble counter where he'd left his sandwich. It was gone. So was his carton of homemade coleslaw. "I . . . uh . . . had some food I left here," he said, trying to ignore his rumbling stomach.

"What?" Eppie said rudely, like she couldn't believe he was thinking of food at a time like this.

"A sandwich," he said, clearing his throat. "And a carton of coleslaw."

"Oh," Eppie answered vaguely, lowering her swollen and red-rimmed eyes. "I didn't know it was yours. I ate it."

"You *ate* it?" Tucci said incredulously.

"Sorry," Eppie said, stuffing another cookie into

her mouth. "It was only an itty bitty *snack.*" And then, noticing that the detective was not pleased, she burst into sobs again, almost choking on her cookie.

"Goddamn it!" Tucci mumbled under his breath, just as his partner, Lee Eccles—summoned back from a fishing trip—arrived.

"Jeez!" Lee exclaimed. "There's a friggin' circus goin' on outside. What in hell happened here?"

chapter 2

Madison Castelli sat in front of her laptop at the kitchen table, diligently attempting to compose a story about Salli T. Turner. It was not easy. A few days ago she had flown out from her home base, New York, to stay with her old college roommate, TV entertainment reporter Natalie DeBarge, and to conduct an interview with powerful superagent Freddie Leon. On the plane she had been seated next to Salli and they'd started talking. At first Madison considered Salli to be the definitive Hollywood bimbo, but after a while she changed her mind, and they got along fine. Later on, when Salli had found out that Madison worked for the high-concept magazine *Manhattan Style*, she immediately wanted to be in it, so they arranged to get together for an interview.

The day of Salli's brutal murder, Madison had lunched with Salli at her palatial Pacific Palisades mansion, where they acted like a couple of girl-friends, chatting about everyone and everything. Actually, Salli had done most of the talking, while Madison listened—but that's what good journalists did, and Salli certainly had plenty to say.

Now she was dead, and Madison sat at her laptop staring blankly at the screen. She already had gone to Salli's house and told the detective in charge of the investigation everything she knew. She also had given him a copy of the audiotape she'd made of her interview with Salli. He'd said he would listen to it later and call her if there was anything he wanted to discuss with her.

Pushing back her long dark hair, she sighed deeply. In a way, it was probably best to get it all out on paper, yet in another way, she was so upset by Salli's death that she wasn't sure she could remain completely unattached.

Drumming her fingers on the table, she wondered what to say about the girl everybody *thought* they knew but didn't really know at all. Salli T. Turner, the sizzling platinum blonde who regularly appeared on *E.T.* and *Hard Copy,* and was a staple in every tabloid—photographed running into parties, emerging from clubs and discos, clad in revealing tight rubber dresses and exceptionally high heels, her bountiful cleavage always on show. She seemed always to be waving and laughing, her megawatt smile lighting up the night.

And yet, beneath the boobs and abundance of blond hair had lurked a very simple girl, a very *nice* girl. And even though they'd only known each other a short time, Madison had liked her a lot, for Salli had possessed a naivete and freshness which was surprisingly endearing.

Abruptly she closed her laptop. She didn't feel like writing; she felt like crying. This horrific murder was so senseless. *Why* had it taken place? What had Salli done to merit such a frenzy of violence?

Madison knew what she *should* do—forget about the murders and concentrate on Freddie Leon, since he was the main thrust of her trip to L.A., and she'd done virtually nothing about arranging an interview. Of course, the elusive Freddie Leon was notorious for not granting interviews, but Victor Simons, her editor in New York, had assured her he could set it up.

Yeah, Victor, she thought sourly. *When?*

To take her mind off Salli, Madison decided to call Freddie Leon's longtime secretary, Ria Santiago—whose private home number she'd gotten from Freddie's erstwhile partner, Max Steele. She had to stop thinking about Salli; it was all too dark and depressing, and she'd been depressed enough when she'd arrived in L.A.—what with David, her live-in love of two years, walking out on her and immediately marrying his childhood sweetheart. Damn David! Why couldn't he have been honest with her? The cowardly skunk had gone out for a pack of cigarettes and failed to come back. Oh yes, he'd left her a stupid note about how he couldn't deal with commitment, then five weeks later he'd gotten married!

Men! She'd had it with them. Why couldn't she find one like her father, Michael, who at fifty-eight was the best looking and nicest man she knew? He and her stunningly beautiful mother, Stella, had an idyllic marriage. They'd been together thirty years and hardly ever spent a night apart. Madison missed them since they'd given up their elegant New York apartment and moved to Connecticut. It was far too long since she'd spent a weekend with them, and as soon as she was through in L.A., that's exactly what she planned on doing.

Everyone told Madison she was a female version of her father, which secretly pleased her because she adored her dad—he was powerful and charming, two qualities she greatly admired. Besides, she had no desire to compete with her mother, who was fair haired and deliciously feminine. Madison liked being tall and rangy with smooth olive skin, jet-black hair and direct, almond-shaped eyes. And then there were her lips—men fell in love with her lips, which were full and seductive and ever so slightly pouty. However, Madison was a no-nonsense girl who played her looks down and concentrated on being smart. She loved competing with the boys and coming out on top. *Maybe that's what frightened David away,* she thought ruefully. *Couldn't take the competition.*

Before she could punch out Ria Santiago's number, Cole, Natalie's fitness-trainer brother, came into the room. Cole was gay in a fiercely masculine way and much too good-looking for his own good. He'd also known Salli, and like everyone else in L.A. on this quiet Sunday morning he was thinking about her violent death.

"Hey," he said, reaching for the coffeepot.

"Hey," Madison responded.

"Didja go see the detective?" Cole asked, pouring himself a mug of black coffee.

"I sure did."

"Anythin' new?"

"Nothing that I know of."

"It's shit," Cole mumbled, pulling out a chair and sitting down. "Salli didn't deserve to get taken out like that."

"I know," Madison said in somber agreement.

Cole reached for the TV clicker and tuned into the *E* channel, where they were already showing a quickly put together retrospective. There was Salli in red. Salli in blue. Salli in skintight. Salli in her famous black rubber swimsuit. And then the male star of *Teach!* appeared, an actor past his prime, who still thought he was a major stud. "Everyone was in love with Salli," the actor said, Hollywood casual in well-fitting linen pants and a chest-baring silk shirt, his capped teeth catching the light. "Salli was a *very* special person."

Commercial break.

"Would you switch to Natalie's channel?" Madison asked.

Cole obliged. There was Natalie on the screen, vibrantly black and pretty, dressed in a shocking-pink jacket and short white dress. "The Salli everyone knew and loved came from a little town outside of Chicago," Natalie said. "And we have learned from family and friends that ever since Salli took her first steps, she wanted to be an actress."

Cut to baby pictures of Salli. A fat little cutie. And then on came a "friend of the family"—a stone-faced woman with badly dyed red hair and an eyelid twitch. "I knew Salli since she was two years old," croaked the woman, her voice a gin-soaked rasp. "An' to know her was to love her."

"Jesus!" Madison murmured. "They'll be crawling out from everywhere."

"Who?" Cole asked.

"People who met her once in their lives. It's *their* chance for glory."

"Guess you're right."

"It happens every time somebody famous dies."

"Yeah," Cole agreed.

"Where's her family? Her mother?"

Cole rubbed his faintly stubbled chin. "Didn't she tell you about her mom when you interviewed her?"

"She hedged—I didn't pursue."

Cole took a deep breath, his handsome features deadly serious. "Salli's mom was murdered when she was ten. It was her big secret."

Madison felt a cold chill creeping up her spine. "How do you know this?" she asked.

Cole was silent for a moment before replying. "There was a time Salli an' I were pretty close," he said, refusing to make eye contact. "She kinda viewed me as a challenge—y'know, the good-looking guy who wasn't into having sex with her. It drove her nutty. Salli liked to think she could get any man she zeroed in on. Sex was her big validation, her comfort zone."

Madison raised an eyebrow. "And did she get you?"

"We did it once," Cole admitted sheepishly. "For God's sake, *don't* tell Natalie."

"Of course not."

"It was before she got really famous."

"And that's when her then husband, Eddie, became jealous of you?"

"He suspected something was goin' on, even though he knew I was gay. So he made her stop using me as her trainer."

"I don't get it," Madison said, frowning. "If you're totally gay, how did she—"

"Hey," Cole said, throwing up his well-muscled arms. "I'm gay, not dead. And Salli knew exactly what to do to turn me on. She was an expert at sex. It was her game, and man—that girl always played to win."

Madison nodded understandingly. Nothing really surprised her. And Cole was right, Salli *had* gotten off on all the attention.

Cole stood up. "I'm goin' for a hike," he said. "Wanna come?"

She shook her head; everyone was so energetic in L.A. Didn't they know how to relax? "I'll pass," she said. "I'm hoping to interview Freddie Leon's secretary."

"*You*, girl, are missin' out," Cole said, heading for the door. "Nothin' like a good hike in the hills to set your head straight."

"Thanks for the offer," she said, reaching for the coffeepot and refilling her cup. "Maybe some other time."

As soon as he left, Madison called Ria Santiago, identified herself and told the secretary she was writing a piece on Freddie Leon for *Manhattan Style* and would like an opportunity to sit down and talk.

Ria's response was cold. "Does Mr. Leon know about this?"

"I'm hoping to meet with him tomorrow."

Ria: "I doubt it. Mr. Leon does not give interviews."

"I'm sure he'll make an exception."

"I'm sure he won't."

And the bitch hung up.

chapter 3

Kristin Carr sat in front of her dressing-table mirror, staring blankly at her blond and beautiful reflection. She knew that at twenty-three she was undeniably gorgeous, but she also knew that what was reflected was merely her outer image. Inside she was a whore, and she was certain that everyone knew it.

Prostitute, hooker, call girl, whore. All names that described her profession. Not that it was a profession she'd deliberately chosen. No, it was something she'd taken up because it was the only thing she could do to make enough money to keep her sister Cherie at the private nursing home where she had been in a coma for three and a half years—ever since the car accident she'd been in with her so-called boyfriend Howie Powers, the worst kind

15

of Hollywood playboy. Howie had walked away from the head-on crash with nothing but scratches; Cherie had never recovered.

I sell my body for the almighty dollar, Kristin thought sadly. *I allow men to use me any way they want. I'm meat. They devour me. And everyone is happy. Everyone except me.*

The sinister Mister X crossed her mind and she shuddered. His sick demands were beyond mere kinky, but he paid well for the privilege of humiliating her. And that's why her madam, Darlene, had phoned the night before, leaving a message on her machine that Mister X had asked to see her again—even though she'd been with him earlier that same evening.

The problem was that Kristin had taken it upon herself to have a life—much as her inner voice had warned her not to. Instead of listening to her gut feeling, she had gone ahead and fallen in lust with Jake Sica—a laid-back, award-winning photographer, whom she had met in Neiman Marcus. One and a half dates later they were in bed, *her* bed, then last night came the phone call from Darlene— loud and clear on her answering machine.

Darlene's voice was amused and excited, because Mister X was a big spender—which meant Darlene made plenty of commission: "Hi, Kristin, sweetie," she had said. "Boy, has Mister X got a hot nut for *you.* Talk about obsession. Can you believe he wants to book you again tonight, *and* he's willing to spring for another five thousand big ones for the privilege. *Twice* in one night! Honey, you've really got it going." A husky giggle. "What's your secret—a mink-lined snatch? Call me back ASAP. The man is waiting."

And lying in bed making love, Kristin had felt Jake shrivel up inside her before he rolled away.

She hadn't known what to say. In fact, neither of them said a word. After a moment or two, Jake got off the bed and hurried into the bathroom.

Punishment, Kristin thought. *Punishment for imagining I could have a life.*

She had reached for her silk robe at the end of the bed, sat up and put it on. Jake had stayed in the bathroom a long time. When he came out he was dressed and ready to leave.

"I forgot," he'd said, hardly able to look at her. "I'm expecting an important call."

Disappointment had flooded over her. Wasn't he even going to discuss it?

So what? she'd thought defensively. *Maybe this is best. What could he say? Excuse me, Kristin, why didn't you tell me you were a hooker?*

Sorry, Jake, I forgot.

"Uh, I'd like to explain," she ventured, hoping for at least a chance to say something—even if it was only an apology.

"No, Kristin, really," he said, anxious to leave. "There's nothing you have to explain to me. Uh— the truth is—your lifestyle and mine—they uh . . . simply don't mesh."

Was that it? Was the nonpaying customer leaving?

"I understand," she said stiffly, thinking that if he didn't want to get into it, he wasn't worth having anyway. "I'll see you around."

"Yeah," he replied. "Guess so." Then he stopped at the door, turned and stared at her accusingly. "I wish you'd told me," he said.

"Why?" she said, filled with hurt.

"Because it's not fair you didn't. I would've used a condom."

The final blow. How *dare* he say that to her, as if she was a common street prostitute. "Fuck you," she'd yelled, suddenly furious. "Fuck *you!*" And she had gotten up, chased after him, slamming the door on his retreating back. Then she went to her dressing table and sat there, staring, staring, staring at her reflection.

When Max Steele, her once-a-month client, phoned in the morning, she had not picked up. Instead she listened to his message as her answering machine recorded it. Max had never done her any harm—in fact, she quite liked him. She didn't know exactly *what* he did, only that he was a big Hollywood player.

"Hey, baby," he said. "This is Max Steele. I've made a decision. I'm taking you out of the business, honey, making you exclusive. You tell me what it'll cost to set you up, and I'll do it." A long pause, then—"I've been thinking about things. I want you to be with me. You see, I need somebody like you around. Somebody to keep me focused. I can introduce you to people and change your life.

Nobody'll know who you are, or what you used to be. This is going to fly, Kristin. Trust me." Another long pause. "I have a meeting at eleven, so call me any time after twelve and we'll work something out. Okay, honey?"

Okay, honey, she thought. *I can do that. If you want to pay me the kind of money Mister X does, you can have me. Because nobody else wants me. I'm used goods. So, Max Steele, I am all yours.*

chapter 4

"**Y**ou're late," Detective Tucci said to his partner, thoroughly grumpy because the maid had devoured his sandwich—not to mention an entire carton of Faye's homemade coleslaw.

"Hey, buddy, *you* try racin' back from a fishin' trip in the middle of nowhere," Detective Lee Eccles complained, frowning. He was a tall, stoop-shouldered man with a weathered face and exceptionally large hands. "It ain't easy," he grumbled. "An' *then,* when I stopped by the station—my freakin' luck—I got sent out on another homicide. Or a suicide—who the fuck knows? Knockout blond babe washed up on the Malibu shore. Legs from here to Cuba. Forensics are runnin' a check on her now."

20

"You missed the big one here."

"My freakin' luck again. Fill me in. Tell me what we've got."

"Two dead bodies. One female, one male. The female stabbed multiple times. The male shot once in the face. The female's husband arrived home at three A.M. Gave him the news, he shut himself in the bedroom. His lawyer, Marty Steiner, arrived this morning—they've been locked in there together for a couple of hours."

"That piece a shit," Lee spat in disgust.

"You know him?"

"Some freakin' asshole," Lee said, picking at his teeth with a dirty fingernail. "Had dealin's with him before."

Lee Eccles and Detective Tucci had been partners for an uneasy six months. Tucci's previous partner had been a veteran detective, now retired. Lee was smart enough, but too abrasive for Tucci's taste. His favorite off-duty pastime was hanging out in bars and strip clubs, and he constantly talked about women in such graphic terms that he offended Tucci's sensibilities because his remarks were so sexist and derogatory. Tucci had complained once.

"Get yourself to a fuckin' monastery," Lee had responded with a mean scowl.

"What the hell does *that* mean?" Tucci growled, and they almost had gotten into a fistfight.

Since that time they had tolerated each other, but there was no real camaraderie.

"You don't look so good," Lee remarked.

"Didn't get any sleep," Tucci replied. *"And* I'm hungry."

"You're always freakin' hungry," Lee said, impatiently cracking his knuckles. "If you stopped eatin' so damn much, you wouldn't have such a big gut."

"I'm dieting," Tucci admitted, stung by the criticism.

Lee guffawed. "Yeah, until the next donut comes along!"

Tucci didn't bother answering. His gut wasn't *that* bad—Faye said she loved cuddling up to him. "You're huggable," she often said. *Hmm* . . . he thought, it would be nice if she changed that to "fuckable." Not that they had any problems in that department—although she *had* told him he was getting too heavy when he was on top, making love to her. Hence the diet.

"What's the deal?" Lee said impatiently. "We gonna wait 'til the husband decides to come out an' speak to us? Whyn't you go knock on the door an' tell him we need t' interview him *now."*

Lee was right for once, Tucci thought. He definitely had had enough of sitting in this house of death. Still, he had to do it by the book. "Bobby Skorch doesn't *have* to talk to us," he pointed out. *"You* know that."

"He'll talk. For your info, when I was over at the station I took a gander at the ex. The dumb jerk is sittin' in a cell sweatin' it. Apparently he called his lawyer, who ain't exactly breakin' a leg to bail him."

"Really?" Tucci said.

"Yeah, and you'd better get your fat butt outside an' make some bullshit announcement to the media," Lee said. "The natives are gettin' ornery, nearly pulled me to pieces on my way in. An' while you're out there, take a look at the ass on that little Chinese chick from channel four. Now *she's* a piece! I wouldn't mind reamin' it up *that* juicy rear." Tucci threw him a disapproving look and Lee chuckled heartily. "What's your problem? Don't wanna get it up with anyone 'cept Faye?"

"Do me a favor," Tucci said, clenching his teeth and willing himself to remain calm. "Leave my wife out of this conversation."

"Oh, yeah, yeah—your wife," Lee said mockingly. "Faye's too fuckin' good to mention." A ribald laugh. "Face it, Tucci, she's got your balls in a lather an' your dick strapped to her left tit."

"That's enough," Tucci said, his face reddening. He knew that Faye and Lee had a history of sorts. She'd gone on a date with Lee once, long before she met him, and Lee had behaved badly. She wouldn't reveal the details, but suffice to say that whenever Lee's name came up she made a disgusted face.

"Yeah, yeah," Lee said, cracking his knuckles again. "So show me where you found the dead broad. Shit, I'm sorry I missed out on *this* babe. Wouldn't've minded an in-the-flesh close-up of *those* tits."

Tucci decided he'd had enough. As soon as he could, he was making an appointment to see Captain Marsh and requesting a new partner.

chapter 5

Diana Leon pulled up outside the Four Seasons, left her car with a parking valet, and entered the hotel. She felt oddly apprehensive. It was the first time she would be with Max Steele on her own. And yet, why not? Max and Freddie had worked together for many years, and she'd always had a friendly relationship with her husband's partner—although deep down she knew it was more than that, and now it was time they both voiced something that was becoming painfully obvious.

Yes, Max, she hoped she had the courage to say. *I'm married to Freddie, but it's a marriage in name only. And since you're not attached to anybody right now, and you're departing I.A.A., I suggest that I leave Freddie and come with you.*

25

Diana was forty-three years old and this was the boldest move she'd ever made. She had been married to Freddie for fifteen years. Now, finally, she was doing something on her own without getting Freddie's permission.

She giggled nervously to herself, feeling like a silly schoolgirl. If Max was in agreement, *could* she leave Freddie? *Would* she leave? The situation was in Max's hands; she would have to feel her way carefully.

"Mrs. Leon," the maitre d' greeted her warmly. "How nice to welcome you again to the Four Seasons. Mr. Steele is waiting."

Oh, God! She was having breakfast with Max Steele, a notorious womanizer. What must people think?

As she approached the table, Max stood up to greet her. She experienced a fleeting moment of sheer panic. Max was so unlike Freddie, who was always in control. Max was an unpredictable wild card and he excited the hell out of her.

"Hi, Diana," Max said.

She noticed that his hair was slightly mussed in a most attractive way, and that his suntan, as usual, was glowing. He was dressed all in white from his pristine pants to his casual summer cashmere sweater.

"Hello, Max," she said, hoping that she'd picked the right outfit. The girls he dated were always outrageously underdressed in flimsy little mini-dresses and barely there tank tops. This morning, after much thought, she had chosen a Calvin Klein blue blazer, worn over a pale-blue silk shirt and beige linen slacks. Casual, elegant and under-stated—that was her look and she wore it well.

"I was kind of surprised to get your call," Max said.

"Well," she answered, choosing her words care-fully as she sat down, "I was surprised and upset about what happened last night."

Max nodded his agreement. "Yeah—that hus-band of yours," he said, picking up a coffee spoon and tapping it on the table. "Couldn't say what he had to say in private. Had to do it in front of that fucking—I'm sorry, in front of Ariel. She's not my favorite person."

"Nor mine either," Diana said quickly. "In fact, if it was up to me, I wouldn't have her in my house. She's duplicitous. I'm sure she got to where she is by sleeping with Billy Cornelius."

Max laughed. *"C'mon,* Diana," he teased. "I've never heard you talk like that about people. You're always Miss Straightlaced."

"Is that what you think of me, Max?" she said, giving him a bold look.

Max was no fool; he caught the signals. Diana Leon was flirting with him. "Uh . . . never really thought about it," he said, wondering where this was leading. The waiter came over and hovered by their table, order pad in hand. "What'll you have, honey?" Max asked.

She liked the way he called her "honey." It was casual, yet extremely intimate. "Maybe some tea."

"No toast? Eggs? Waffles?"

"No, just tea. Earl Grey," she said, speaking directly to the waiter.

"The lady wants tea," Max said. "And bring me another orange juice, two eggs, sunny-side up, one slice of crisp bacon, three pieces of toast, not too well done, and more coffee."

"Yes, Mr. Steele," said the waiter.

"So," Max said, leaning back and surveying the room. "What can I do for you, Diana?"

You can ravish me, she longed to say. *You can take me to bed and do all the things to me that you do to your numerous girlfriends. And I will love you, care for you and be the faithful woman forever by your side.*

"I wanted to say, Max, that whatever happens, you have my full support."

"That's good to know," he said, his wandering eyes checking out a pretty brunette with long tanned legs on her way out of the dining room. "The truth is, Diana, I changed my mind."

"You changed your mind?" she repeated, not sure what he'd changed his mind about.

"Freddie and I have been through so much together; there's no way I can leave the firm. I simply can't do it to him."

The waiter returned and refilled Max's coffee cup.

Diana waited until he had left before speaking.

"I'm sure you're aware that in the *Times* today there's a story about you taking over at Orpheus Studios," she said.

"It's all bullshit," Max said sharply. "They write these stories before anything's signed. I spoke to Billy Cornelius this morning and told him the deal is off."

"You *did?*"

"Yes, honey. Y'know, on reflection, I reckon I was going through some kind of midlife crisis thing. Freddie'll understand."

"But, Max, if you feel you can do better elsewhere, then you *should* move," she said, a slight tinge of desperation creeping into her voice.

"Hey, hey—" Max said, with a half smile. "Don't encourage me."

"I'm encouraging you to be yourself," Diana said, her expression earnest.

"Did Freddie send you?" he asked curiously.

"No, he didn't," she responded indignantly. "As a matter of fact, Freddie failed to come home last night. I have no idea where he was. He walked in when I was leaving this morning, looking dishevelled."

Max stared at her disbelievingly. "Freddie, dishevelled?"

"Yes, Freddie."

"Don't tell me he's got a broad . . . I mean, no disrespect to you, Diana."

"There's no one else, Max," she said confidently.

"If you say so . . ."

29

"The truth is," she leaned toward him, lowering her voice to a whisper, "Freddie doesn't like sex."

"Doesn't like sex, huh?" Max said, storing that little piece of information away for future use.

"I can speak to you in the strictest confidence, can't I?"

"Sure, baby," Max said agreeably. Hey, bonding with Freddie's wife was a kick. This way he could get the inside track on everything.

Diana wondered if she had said too much. No. Why *shouldn't* she confide in Max? He would never betray her. "Freddie's not a sexual being," she said. A long, meaningful pause. "But *I* am . . ."

Oh, Jesus. Was she coming on to him? Freddie's uptight wife? No way. And yet . . . she had that predatory look, a look Max knew only too well. Women on the make . . . he'd had more of those than he cared to remember. Usually actresses. Hey, it wasn't *his* fault if he was irresistible to women.

"Diana," he said carefully. "I'm not sure you should be here with me."

Her slate gray eyes stared boldly into his. "Why not?"

"Because . . . uh . . ." he began, thinking fast, it wouldn't do to insult her by telling her he wasn't interested. "Because I . . . uh . . . well, I guess I'm very attracted to you," he lied.

Her face lit up. He had said the right thing. "You *are?*"

"Yes, Diana, honey. But, believe me, this is not the time for either of us to do anything about it."

"Why not?" she demanded, bedroom eyes materializing out of nowhere.

Oh, shit! She wasn't going to give up easy.

"Trust me. It's not."

Tentatively she reached across the table, placing her hand gently over his. "I've waited so long for this moment, Max. Something told me it was inevitable."

He slid his hand out from under hers, indicating the approaching waiter with his eyebrows. "Be cool, Diana," he said in a low voice. "The tabs have spies everywhere. You're an important Hollywood wife—you're news. So am I right now. We shouldn't even be seen together like this."

"I know," she said. "But for once I don't want to do the right thing. I want to do what makes me happy."

Freddie's wife was on a roll. *Jesus!* What had he done to deserve *this?*

"Diana," he said, attempting a serious voice. "I have too much regard and respect for you to allow you to jeopardize your future."

"What do you mean?"

"We all know Freddie has a vindictive streak. If he even suspected you had eyes for another man . . ."

"I don't care," she said stubbornly.

"I do. I'm trying to protect you here."

"When I'm with you, Max, I don't need protecting."

This kind of response was exactly what he *didn't*

need. "You might *think* you don't," he said sternly. "But trust me, you do."

He imagined Freddie's face if Diana went to him and informed her husband she was running off with Max Steele. The shit wouldn't just hit the fan, it would explode all the way from Beverly Hills to Bel Air. Christ! How to get out of this one?

Then it came to him. The perfect solution. "Diana," he said, with a perfectly straight face. "I think you should be the first to know. Last night I got engaged."

chapter 6

Freddie Leon thought of himself as an in-control and reasonable man, but in view of what had happened over the last twenty-four hours, he could not remain calm. His faithful partner Max Steele had betrayed him, and it infuriated Freddie that Max had manipulated him in such a way. The disloyal son-of-a-bitch.

Freddie stood under the powerful jets of his shower, soaking his body. After a night away from home he felt the need to thoroughly cleanse himself. Hotel rooms disgusted him—however luxurious. The late Howard Hughes had had the right idea, covering his shoes with Kleenex and walking around with a hospital mask over half his face.

Last night Freddie had known he had to get out of the house. He had no desire to lie in bed beside

Diana, listening to her nag about how he had ruined her dinner party.

Through the noise of the shower he heard the phone ring, and to his annoyance no one picked up. He stepped out of the shower and answered it himself. It was Ria. "Yes?" he snapped, wondering why his secretary was bothering him on a Sunday.

"Mr. Leon," Ria said. "Are you aware there's a woman from *Manhattan Style* magazine in town? She's been sent out here from New York to write a piece on you. In fact, she fully expects you to grant her an interview."

"Excuse me?" Freddie said irritably.

"Madison Castelli. She's here to conduct an exclusive interview with you."

"Why me?" Freddie said, frowning.

"You're very high profile, Mr. Leon." As if she had to explain it to him. Freddie Leon knew exactly how important and powerful he was. "So I'm to presume you don't know anything about this?"

"No, I don't," he said, annoyed she'd seen fit to disturb him at home. "How do *you* know?"

"Ms. Castelli called me herself."

"Where did she get your number?"

"I didn't ask. I merely informed her you would not be interested."

"Right. She'll get no cooperation from me, so if she's smart she'd better quit now."

"With all due respect, Mr. Leon, you cannot tell the press what they can and can't do."

"I can tell them what I like," Freddie snapped and put the phone down. "Diana," he yelled. "Diana!" There was no response, so wrapping a towel around his waist, he walked from his bathroom into the bedroom. Then he remembered; Diana had gone out. "Damn!" he mumbled under his breath. He hated it when his wife exhibited attitude and wasn't around to attend to his needs. He sat on the edge of the bed and decided to give Ariel Shore a call.

When Ariel came to the phone she was suitably cool, which annoyed him even more. He had a good relationship with Ariel and did not want anything spoiling it.

"I guess we're the last to know," Ariel said, her tone icy.

"What do you mean?" Freddie asked.

"Didn't you see the *L.A. Times* this morning?"

"I haven't read the papers yet."

"Take a look. Your partner made an announcement, or somebody made an announcement for him."

"How could that happen?"

"*Exactly,* Freddie," Ariel said triumphantly, as if she'd caught him cheating at cards. "How *could* it happen without either of us knowing about it? *We're* supposed to be Hollywood insiders. *We're* supposed to know everything weeks before anything takes place."

"Ariel, I—"

"Anyway," she rudely interrupted. "I went to see Billy this morning."

"You did?"

"I thought it was time I settled this nonsense."

"What happened?"

"I told Billy he could not hire *anyone* without asking me. And if you're as clever as I *know* you are, when Max comes crawling back, you'll immediately terminate your partnership."

"You don't have to tell me what to do, Ariel," Freddie said, pissed that she would even try. "That was already my plan."

"Good, because my studio does not care to conduct business with anyone who has anything at all to do with Max Steele."

"Point taken, Ariel," Freddie said. And as far as he was concerned, that was the end of Max Steele.

chapter 7

Madison had finished writing her piece on Salli T. Turner. She didn't consider it up to her usual standard, but she knew that she was too emotionally involved to be able to do any better. She faxed a copy of the article to Victor in New York, then immediately wished she hadn't. Victor responded quickly. He phoned and told her it was good.

"Not good enough," she answered, an expert at putting herself down. "Do I have time to do a rewrite?"

"No," Victor said firmly. "The piece is excellent. Stop being so critical."

When Cole returned from his hike, he suggested to Madison that he take her out for lunch. "We'll grab a Neil McCarthy salad at the Beverly Hills Hotel," he said persuasively.

"I don't know," she demurred, feeling guilty at the thought of going out to lunch while Salli lay brutally murdered. "I'm not in the mood."

"C'mon," Cole urged. "It'd make *me* feel better to get out. An' if Natalie's around, I'll even take her."

She stood up and stretched. "Natalie's having lunch with Luther."

"Who's Luther?"

"An ex-football player she met at Jimmy's house last night."

"Straight?"

"Of course."

Cole grinned. "Shame!"

Madison couldn't help laughing. "Okay," she said, deciding it might be good to get out after all. "We're on for lunch. You talked me into it."

"Didn't have to do much talkin'," Cole said with a friendly wink.

"So what did you do?" Jimmy Sica asked his brother, who had just gotten through telling him what had happened between him and Kristin the night before.

"I left," Jake said. "What would *you* have done under those circumstances?"

"Jesus!" Jimmy said, shaking his head. "It would've shocked the crap outta me. And she seemed so . . . gorgeous."

"She was gorgeous all right," Jake said grimly. "Five-thousand-a-night gorgeous."

They were standing in the middle of their father's bungalow at the Beverly Hills Hotel, waiting for him to emerge from the bedroom so they could escort him to his wedding ceremony, which was to take place in the lavish gardens.

"What a scam!" Jimmy exclaimed. "D'you think she was planning on charging *you?*"

"Of course not," Jake said sharply, already regretting telling his brother. "We had a good thing going."

"So you think if the phone deal hadn't happened, you wouldn't have found out?"

"That's exactly right."

"Did you use a—"

"Nope."

"Well, buddy, *you* had better get yourself tested pronto."

"I plan to."

Jimmy flopped down on the couch, legs splayed. "There's no way you could've known. The hookers in L.A. are the best-looking broads in town."

"How would *you* know?"

"I get around, little bro'."

Jake couldn't stop pacing up and down. "She seemed like such a sweetheart," he said. "Innocent . . . clean-cut . . ."

"Where exactly did you meet her?"

"In the men's department at Neiman Marcus."

"Ha!" Jimmy exclaimed. "That should've given you a clue. What was she doing *there?*"

"Sitting at the martini bar. *I* picked *her* up, it wasn't as if *she* was coming on to *me.*"

"That's what *you* thought," Jimmy muttered darkly.

"D'you think I overreacted?" Jake asked.

"Are you shitting me?" Jimmy said, making a face. "She's a *hooker* for crissake."

"I hope you're not speaking about my future bride," their father, Cosmos, said, emerging from the bedroom clad in a John Travolta *Saturday Night Fever* three-piece white suit and a screamingly bright red tie. He was a handsome man, but at least sixty pounds overweight, which caused his three-piece suit to bulge in all the wrong places.

"No way, Dad," Jimmy said, attempting to conceal his amusement at his father's outrageous outfit.

Cosmos Sica was sixty-two years old with a shock of silver hair, matching moustache and a wily grin. The woman he was about to marry was a twenty-year-old manicurist from San Diego who was to be his fourth wife. Jimmy and Jake were used to their high-living dad, and as far as they were concerned, the old guy could do what he liked—and typically he did. Cosmos was smart enough in business that it was okay for him to be stupid about women. And if he could afford them, why not?

"You look good, Dad," Jake lied, knowing his father craved compliments.

"An' you don't look so bad yourself, son," Cosmos said, admiring himself in a wall mirror. "Isn't it about time you found yourself a regular girl?"

"He did," Jimmy said with a slight smirk.

"Good," Cosmos said loudly. "It's not healthy for a man to be by himself. You need a warm body to snuggle up with at night."

"She's not exactly someone I'm planning on spending the rest of my life with," Jake said, throwing Jimmy a warning look.

"Shall I tell him?" Jimmy said, starting to laugh.

"No way," Jake objected.

"Tell me what?" Cosmos asked, brushing the edge of his moustache with his fingers. "This is my wedding day—you can tell me anything."

"He fell in love with a hooker," Jimmy announced, unable to stop himself.

"He did *what?*" Cosmos yelled.

"He thought she was a nice girl," Jimmy said. "It turned out she was a nice girl all right—the kinda nice girl you *pay.*"

Cosmos roared with hearty laughter. "Nothing wrong with a pretty girl making an honest living. That's what I say."

Jake glared at his brother. "Quit making my business public knowledge."

"I'm your father, for crissake," Cosmos boomed. "What's with the public knowledge? You know you can trust me; it'll go no further."

Sure, Jake thought glumly, *knowing Dad, everyone will be in on the joke by the end of the wedding. Damn Jimmy and his big mouth.*

Jimmy hauled himself off the couch. "We ready?" he said.

Cosmos nodded vigorously. "You bet!" he said, almost popping a button on his vest. "Fourth time lucky, huh? Come on, boys, I'm impatient to get to my wedding night!"

In spite of a huge and expensive face-lift there was something about the lobby of the Beverly Hills Hotel that screamed old Hollywood. "I keep on expecting to bump into Clark Gable or Lana Turner," Madison joked, glancing around.

"I know what you mean," Cole said. "This place has history."

"It sure does," she agreed.

"C'mon," he said, taking her arm. "We're eating on the terrace of the Polo Lounge. You ever had a Neil McCarthy salad?"

"Sounds vaguely communistic."

"The best chopped salad you'll ever have."

"You're so knowledgeable," she teased. "And to think—Natalie and I were both under the impression you'd end up being a gang member."

"Right," Cole drawled. "Instead, I'm a politically incorrect gay guy who knows everyone's secrets."

"You do?"

42

"I sure do."

"Are there any more secrets about Salli?"

"Maybe," he said mysteriously.

Madison let it drop; she knew when to push and when not to. "So, Cole," she said lightly. "What's *your* love life like? You seeing anyone special?"

"Haven't gotten that lucky—yet," he said ruefully. "So I keep playing the field. 'Course it drives Natalie insane. She's convinced I'll get AIDS and then she'll have to look after me. And you know how *that* would piss her off."

"She's always adored you, Cole. When we were at college together she was always talking about you and worrying that you were okay."

"Yeah," he laughed. "I know, I know. She sure loves her baby brother."

"How did she take it when you told her you were gay?"

"Y'know, she was kinda cool. It was my parents who freaked. An' it was Nat who talked 'em around."

As they continued walking through the lobby, Madison spotted two vaguely familiar faces coming toward her. She thought about taking evasive action, but it was too late. Jimmy Sica had seen her.

"Madison!" he said, flashing his perfect anchorman smile. "What are *you* doing here?"

"I could ask *you* the same question."

"It's our dad's wedding," Jimmy explained, gesturing toward Cosmos. "Allow me to introduce you to the man himself. We're on our way to his execution—fourth one."

Cosmos took her hand, squeezing it tightly. "Delighted to meet such a lovely woman," he said, oozing charm before turning to Jake and inquiring *sotto voce,* "Is this the young lady you were telling us about?"

"No," Jake said quickly. "Madison's a journalist from New York."

"I love it when I get billing," Madison said, with a nod in his direction. "Do you all know Cole, Natalie's brother?"

"So *you're* the famous fitness guru," Jimmy said, shaking Cole's hand. "Natalie keeps on telling me you're the best in town."

"The best what?" Cole said, grinning cheekily.

"The best guy to get my pathetic abs in shape," Jimmy said, grinning back.

"I can do that," Cole said.

"Stop flirting," Madison scolded. "They're both straight, or at least I *think* they are." Her eyes met Jake's. "How was your date last night?"

"Casual," he answered. "Nothing serious."

"Why don't you two drop by the wedding?" Jimmy suggested.

"We're on our way to lunch," Madison explained. "Besides, we're not exactly dressed for a wedding."

"You look great to me," Jake said.

Jimmy's attention was taken by a woman in a

blue jogging outfit who wanted his autograph. He loved being recognized, especially in front of his father, who was duly impressed.

"Hey, I'm sorry last night kind of, uh . . . ended abruptly," Jake said.

"That's all right," Madison answered, thinking that her first impression from last night had not been wrong; he was very attractive in a sexy, laid-back way. "It was abrupt for all of us."

"Bad news about Salli. You knew her, didn't you?"

"Yes, it's so sad. She was a sweet person. You might not realize it from her public image, but she was."

"You wouldn't be free for dinner tonight, would you?" Jake asked impulsively.

"Uh . . ." She tried to think of an excuse, but none came to mind.

"She's free," Cole said, answering for her.

"Well, yes, I guess I am," she said, shooting Cole a "mind-your-own-business" look.

"Pick you up at seven?" Jake said.

"Let's go," Cosmos boomed. "I got a wedding to attend. An' a bride to make happy!"

"Lots of luck, Mr. Sica," Madison said.

"It's not luck I need, pretty lady," Cosmos said, roaring with laughter again. "It's stamina. An' plenty of it!"

The three of them walked off.

"That's *you* settled for tonight," Cole said, pleased with himself for interfering.

"What made you think I *wanted* to go out with him?" she asked irritably.

"He seems like a cool dude—go for it."

"What?"

"Hey—if I can't have him, why shouldn't you?"

"Cole," she said sternly. "You railroaded me into that."

"No way."

"You did," she said accusingly. "I'm not sure he even *wanted* to ask me out."

"Then how come he did?"

"Oh, God! How do I know?"

"Maddy," Cole interrupted. *"You* are *totally* fine. So go—have yourself a good time, an' stop worryin'."

"Now you sound like Natalie."

He arched an amused eyebrow. "Somethin' wrong with that?"

She took his arm. "Okay, matchmaker, let's go get lunch. I'm starving!"

chapter 8

At exactly noon Kristin picked up the phone and called Max.

He answered immediately. "Perfect timing," he said, sounding excessively cheery. "You're an engaged woman."

"Excuse me?" she said, wondering what he was up to now.

"Don't worry," he said. "It's a paying job. You'll be my fiancée for a while. What do you think of *that?*"

"I think you're crazy, Max," she said with a sigh. "But then that's nothing new."

"Don't you like my idea?"

"I'll repeat what I just said. You're crazy."

"Can you come over?"

She'd never been to his house, and yet, if he wanted her to move in, she certainly had to check it out. "Where do you live?"

"I'll give you the address. Be here in an hour."

"I can't do that," she said quickly. "I have somewhere to go first. I could be there around four."

"Where are you going?"

"We haven't done the deal yet, Max," she said sharply. "So don't question me."

"Okay, okay," he answered, soothing her with his voice. "But, honey, believe me—this is gonna be a cool situation."

She was resigned to her fate—whatever it might be. "If you say so."

"I *know* so," he assured her, and then he gave her his address in Bel Air. She replaced the receiver and sighed deeply, wondering if she was making the right move. What did she really know about Max Steele? He was just another client, that's all. Why was she even considering such a radical move?

All she could think about was Jake. They'd had such a strong connection, or so she'd thought. And then her stupid answering machine and Darlene's message had ruined everything.

She had known she would get screwed by Mister X, one way or another.

She went to her closet and picked out the simplest clothes she possessed. Then she pulled her long blond hair back into a ponytail and did not bother putting on makeup.

It was time to visit her sister.

The drive to the nursing home took about an hour. Kristin liked to play books on tape, usually biographies; it gave her something to talk about with clients who were into conversation. Right now she was listening to Robert Evans's *The Kid Stays in the Picture*. He had led a fascinating life—businessman, movie star, head of a studio, grand producer in the great Hollywood tradition. Recently she read that he'd had a stroke and then a few weeks later had gotten married for the fourth time. Then had *that* marriage annulled! Hollywood survivors—they were a breed unto themselves!

She wondered what Jake was doing. He must be at his father's wedding by now, wearing the tie she'd picked out and having such a good time that he'd probably forgotten all about her. She couldn't help remembering his final words: *I wish you'd told me. . . . I would've used a condom.*

How could he say something so hurtful? As if she would ever have put him at risk!

She found it impossible to concentrate on Bob Evans, so she put on the radio instead. A newscaster was talking about the murder of Salli T. Turner. Kristin had never met her, although she'd had several encounters with her wild husband, Bobby Skorch. Bobby was a notorious womanizer, and loved call girls. She had attended several parties where he'd performed quite publicly—even though everyone knew he had a famous wife at home. Bobby was into showing it off, and he had plenty to show: he was one of the most well-endowed men Kristin had ever seen. So well-endowed, in fact, that several of the girls refused to have sex with him—Kristin being one of them.

She remembered after one particular party Darlene had lectured her the next day. *"Never* turn down a client," Darlene had said, practically tut-tutting her annoyance. "It's bad for business."

"He's a tattooed freak," Kristin had replied. "And I don't ever have to do anything I don't want to."

Kristin could not stomach hearing about Salli T. Turner's particularly brutal murder, so she switched stations. A newscaster was speaking about President Clinton, Kenneth Starr and all the goings-on in Washington.

Hollywood and Washington—the men in both cities were beyond horny. Kristin was well aware it was all about power and control. Politicians and movie stars—these men had so much that sometimes the only way they could get off was relinquishing both.

She switched stations again. A news reporter droned on about another murder.

"The body of a young woman was washed up on the Malibu shore this morning. Identity unknown. The only description so far is that the victim was Caucasian and blond. Detectives are investigating."

Two murders. Two blondes.

Another normal Sunday in L.A.

When Kristin arrived at the nursing home, she was greeted warmly by the nurses at the desk. "How's Cherie doing?" she asked, handing over a large bag filled with candy, all the current magazines and a couple of best-selling novels. It was good to keep the nurses happy—that way they'd be sure to give Cherie special attention.

"Same as ever," Mariah, the fat, black, friendly nurse, replied. "No change."

"You never know," Kristin said hopefully. "One of these days she might open her eyes, like Sleeping Beauty."

"Yeah, baby—keep on thinking that way," Mariah said, oozing her large frame out from behind the desk.

"That's why I come here every week," Kristin said. "My voice gets through to her—I know it does. She has to realize *someone* cares."

"You're lookin' pale today," Mariah said, crinkling her eyes. "Everything okay with you, hon?"

"I'm fine," she said quickly. "Too many patients this week." Early on she had told all the nurses that she worked as a dental assistant.

"Ugh! Dunno how you do it," Mariah said. "Staring into all those sloppy mouths. It'd drive *me* loco."

"Somebody's got to do it," Kristin said, anxious to see Cherie.

"Bet all your patients fall in love with you," Mariah said with a saucy wink. "You sure are pretty 'nuff."

"I'm there to do a job, that's all," Kristin said, thinking *ain't that the truth*.

"Yeah, yeah," Mariah said disbelievingly. "Didja catch *Lethal Weapon 4* yet? What a movie! I'm hot for that Chris Rock. Skinny an' sexy! Wouldn't mind spendin' a night in *his* company."

Kristin summoned up a laugh. "Yes, he is cute," she said. Actually she had no idea who Chris Rock was.

"Cute?" Mariah exclaimed. "Honey bun, he's a *horny* hound dog!"

Kristin followed Mariah into her sister's private room and stared down at Cherie—a shadow of the beauty she once had been, kept alive on a machine. It broke her heart every time she saw her.

"Hi, baby," she said, sitting on the edge of the hospital bed and taking her sister's hand, which was ice cold. "It's Kristin. How are you today?"

No response. There was never any response. But she'd stay for an hour and keep talking.

Maybe one day she would get a reaction. She had to keep trying.

If she gave up, all hope would be lost.

chapter 9

Marty Steiner emerged from Bobby Skorch's bedroom at noon, made his way downstairs and confronted the two detectives in the front hall.

"We're ready to ask Mr. Skorch a few questions," Detective Tucci said, asserting himself.

"I'm sure," Marty Steiner replied, smooth as a one-eyed snake. "Fact is, he's too upset to talk to you right now. And I'm requesting that you vacate the premises."

"We still have things to do here," Tucci pointed out. "This *is* a crime scene."

"I think you've had enough time to collect all the evidence you need," Marty Steiner said. "Mr. Skorch would like you and your partner to leave immediately. This is an extremely difficult time, and Mr. Skorch does not need to deal with having his house invaded."

"I'll remind you again—this *is* a crime scene," Tucci said, hating the sleek lawyer and everything he represented.

"Yeah," Lee said, joining in. "It's a goddamn crime scene, for crissake. You think we *wanna* be here?"

Marty Steiner's face gave not a flicker of recognition in Lee's direction. "If you wish to stay, you'll need a warrant," he said calmly. "The bodies have been removed. As I said before, you've had ample time to collect your evidence. Now I want you people out of here."

"Are you telling me that Mr. Skorch has nothing to say to us?" Lee said, belligerent as ever.

"That's correct, Detective."

"Where was he last night?" Lee asked, getting right in the lawyer's face.

"On his way back from Vegas."

"He didn't arrive here 'til three," Lee said accusingly.

"I'm sure you're aware that it's a four- or five-hour drive."

"His *wife* was murdered," Tucci said. "Doesn't he have any questions for *us?*"

"Mr. Skorch has a funeral to prepare for," Marty Steiner said, his voice hardening. "Now unless you have a warrant, I insist you vacate at once."

Tucci and Lee exchanged glances. "I knew he was an asshole," Lee mumbled under his breath.

"Nothing we can do," Tucci said.

"Why *wouldn't* Skorch talk to us?" Lee muttered. "I'm gonna check on his alibi. I wanna know exactly what time he left the hotel in Vegas, an' who was in the car with him. He probably got back here early, found his wife with a guy an' lost it."

"If that was the case," Tucci said, ever the voice of reason, "where's the other man? Why hasn't he come forward?"

"Would *you* under these circumstances? The jerk must've run for his life."

"We'd better go," Tucci said, thinking to himself that maybe on the way back to the station he could stop by a diner and grab a bite to eat.

Lee shrugged. "Fine with me. I came to this case late. If *I'd* gotten to the prick when he arrived back from Vegas, I'd have questioned him then and there."

"He knew his rights," Tucci said, choosing to ignore the fact that Lee was criticizing him. "He was aware he didn't have to talk to me."

"The asshole's guilty," Lee muttered. "Fuckin' guilty."

On his way back to the station, Tucci stopped at Fatburger and devoured a couple of hamburgers with everything. Then he indulged himself with a side order of French fries and onions. There was no way he would confess to Faye that he ate all that food—she'd be too angry. He'd lie, tell her he grabbed a salad.

Back at the station he remembered Madison Castelli's tape and decided to give it a listen. He found it most informative, hearing Salli T. Turner tell about her life. She had a lovely voice—young and vibrant.

Tucci's thoughts kept flashing on her dead body, the vicious cuts and lacerations, the sheer fury the murderer had wreaked upon his victim.

Ah, the price of fame, he thought. Was it worth it? Not for Salli T. Turner.

Later in the day he went down to the morgue to inspect the body of the "Mystery Malibu blonde" as the media were calling the latest victim. The media were having a field day. First the celebrated Salli T. Turner, and now an unknown beautiful blonde washed up on the Malibu shore. Movie star territory. Two murders in as many days. Ratings were zooming.

The mystery blonde was young and lovely. Probably no more than nineteen or twenty, Tucci figured. What happened to her that she ended up dead?

"We're tracking her dental records," Lee informed him. "Should have something by tomorrow."

Tucci shook his head. There was so much violence in the world, so much anger. He picked up the phone and called Faye. "I'll be home late tonight, sweetheart," he said.

"I'm not surprised," she said. "Salli T. Turner is

all over the television. What a terrible tragedy. They're comparing her death to the Nicole Simpson murder."

"They would."

"Don't think about it," Faye said. "Solve it."

"I plan to," Tucci answered.

"Did you enjoy the sandwich?"

He didn't have the heart to tell her that the maid had eaten it. "Delicious," he lied.

"How about the coleslaw?"

"Even more delicious. Almost as delicious as you."

"You're such a flatterer," she said, chuckling happily. "Did you meet with that woman from *Manhattan Style*—Madison Castelli?"

"Yes. She brought me an audiotape of her interview with Salli."

"Have you played it?"

"I was listening to it now."

"Anything useful?"

"It sounds to me like Salli had a real problem with her ex. I'll question him shortly."

"Has he been arrested?"

"Yes. We brought him in on parking violations."

"I miss you," Faye said wistfully.

"Miss you, too," Tucci replied.

"I could make you your favorite pasta tonight," she said, playing the temptress. "Special treat 'cause you've been so good."

The two burgers had made him uncomfortably full, not to mention totally guilty. "That'd be nice," he said, not quite as enthusiastic as she expected him to be. "I'll call you later."

Lee appeared, eating a jelly donut, the jam dribbling down his pointed chin. "The captain wants to see us," he said, wiping his sugary hands on his pants. "Like pronto."

Tucci got up from behind his desk and followed Lee into their captain's office.

Captain Marsh was exceptionally tall, black and bad tempered. He smoked cheap cigars, sported a halfhearted Afro and needed immediate dental work. "The chief of police called—he'd just heard from the mayor's office," he said, getting straight to the point. "This Salli Turner murder. They need an arrest, an' they need it *now*. Forget about everything else an' work this case hard. I promised the chief we'd have someone in custody within twenty-four hours. If you need extra help—let me know. I'm expectin' immediate results."

There goes dinner, Tucci thought. *Nothing like a little pressure to get you through the day.*

chapter 10

"**I** can't believe you're going out with that Jake guy," Natalie said, rolling her eyes in a disapproving way.

"Last night you thought he was cute," Madison pointed out.

"I also thought he was *available*," Natalie said crisply. "Available and cute is one thing. Available and taken is another."

"Who *says* he's taken?"

"Oh, come *on*, girl!" Natalie said. "Did you *see* the way he hustled that blonde out of sight last night. He was hot for her. I mean *steamin'*."

"Apparently not *that* hot," Madison retorted. "Anyway—wasn't it you who said I should get out and have fun? Take my mind off David the jerk?"

"Yeah, but not if you're jumpin' from one jerk to another," Natalie replied. "That'd be too sad."

"It's a date," Madison said patiently. "I'm not moving in with him."

"Praise the Lord!"

"Don't go getting religious on me."

"If Jake's anything like his brother . . ."

"I thought you *liked* his brother; you dragged me over there for dinner last night."

"That's only 'cause Jimmy and I work together."

"Anyway, I'm seeing him. Big deal. One lousy date."

Natalie threw up her hands. "Okay, okay. I'm only trying to watch out for you."

"How was your lunch with Luther?"

Natalie's pretty face broke into a wide smile. "He is *some* hunk."

"You like him, huh?"

"Understatement, girl. He's big and damn sexy. Makes me feel protected."

"Now it's my turn to wave a warning flag in your face. Don't forget, you, too, are coming out of a lousy relationship. Denzl—remember? So don't get carried away."

Natalie giggled. "This is *such* a buzz!" she said. "I feel like we're back in college, sitting around talking about guys. I mean, aren't we a little *old* for this crap?"

"Yes," Madison agreed, smiling.

"One of these days," Natalie said, "I'd like to be

married with a couple of kids, live in a nice little house by the sea, have a great husband who comes home every night at the same time, *and* watch Oprah!"

"Dream world, Nat," Madison said. "You'd *hate* missing out on the action. You *love* what you do."

"True. But I want to do more than cover the entertainment beat. I am *so* sick of talking about Salli T. Turner. Yeah, she was a big TV star and great looking—if you like silicone. But the girl got herself murdered, and now *I* gotta go on and on eulogizing her. It's enough already. I want to report real news, not sensational Hollywood murders."

"I understand," Madison said. "But, remember, it wasn't Salli's fault she got killed."

"Yeah, I know, it's a tragedy. Truth is—it brings back too many bad memories for me."

Madison nodded sympathetically, remembering the night in college when Natalie had been attacked and raped by a man who turned out to be a serial killer. They caught the guy, but it had taken Natalie a year to get over it and stop shaking.

"What're you gonna wear tonight?" Natalie asked, hurriedly changing the subject. "Something sexy, I hope."

"I don't do sexy," Madison said straight-facedly.

"You know what would be *really* good for you?"

"What brilliant idea have you come up with now?"

"Use *him* like guys are always using *us*. Throw

some condoms in your bag and have a night of wild sex."

"What're you *talking* about?"

"Guys do it all the time. And my personal opinion is you need one night of mind-blowing sex. Kind of like a revenge fuck."

"Revenge for what?" Madison asked patiently.

"For the way David treated you."

"He did what made him happy. Besides, one-nighters are not my style."

"*Make* it your style. And you're *not* wearing one of your laid-back outfits. Have I got a dress for you!"

"Don't do dresses either," Madison objected.

Natalie wasn't listening. "It's red, short and *veree* sexy. I was saving it for your birthday—but since you're here, it's perfect! Oh yeah, an' you gotta wear your hair down."

"Why are you trying to make me into something I'm not?" Madison asked, exasperated.

"Treat tonight like an adventure. What's to lose?"

Later, both Cole and Natalie sat around watching Madison get ready for the date. She tried to argue, but instead, couldn't help dissolving into laughter as they instructed her. Cole was a whiz with the makeup brushes; he worked on her eyes and lips, then stood back to admire his handiwork. "Kevyn Aucoin—drop dead!" he crowed.

"It's the Madison makeover!" Natalie yelled.

"You're like one of those secretaries with the bun and glasses."

"I don't wear glasses."

"You know what I'm saying. Remove the glasses, let the hair down and *voilà*—you're Sharon Stone!"

"I'm not even blond, Natalie. And I feel ridiculous in this dress."

"But you *look* hot, girl!"

Cole handed her a packet of condoms. "No, thank you," Madison said, shoving them back at him.

"Just in case," Natalie urged. "Maybe Jake'll take you dancing, and you're in his arms, and then there's that wild moment of no return. If that happens you'll be so damn sorry you don't have them with you. 'Cause no glove—no love."

"Now I *really* feel like I'm back in college," Madison said, laughing. "You two are unbelievable."

"Yeah, we're a fun couple, aren't we," Natalie said, impulsively hugging Cole. "Get used to us, 'cause, girl, we're takin' our act on the road!"

"What's *your* plan tonight, Cole?" Madison asked.

"Got a *hot* date."

"Who with?" Natalie demanded.

"Your favorite," Cole said. "Mr. Mogul."

"Oh, God," Natalie groaned. "Don't you *get* it yet—those power guys are into using and abusing buff young things like you. They're worse than playboys who try to get one over on women."

"I wish you'd meet him. He's a nice guy."

"Nice guy, my ass," Natalie snorted. "He's a billionaire gay caballero who'll use you big time."

"You're prejudiced," Cole said, narrowing his eyes. "You'd sooner see me settle in with a nice boring accountant."

"I don't care what you do. Your lifestyle doesn't bother me."

"Liar! You wish I was straight."

"Can you two quit fighting," Madison said, placing her hands on her slender hips, wishing she could get out of tonight's date with Jake.

Too late. The doorbell rang, and both Cole and Natalie began shoving her toward the door.

No backing out now.

chapter 11

"What are *you* in such a bad mood about?" Freddie asked irritably.

"I'm not," Diana replied, although she obviously was.

"And where *were* you this morning?" he added, annoyed that she hadn't been around to tend to his every need.

"Why do you care?" Diana said, her face flushed. "I didn't ask where *you* were last night."

He threw her a warning look. "Don't get pissy with me, Diana."

"Why *did* you leave?" she continued, determined not to be intimidated. "You know I'm not happy alone in the house."

"You weren't alone. You had dozens of caterers around."

66

"Oh, *please.*"

"Do you have any idea how much these dinner parties of yours cost me?"

"As if you care," Diana said, exasperated. "It's all tax deductible." She stalked into the kitchen and poured herself a cup of coffee. It was difficult for her to get over the shock of Max's engagement. Unbearable timing, yet she *still* couldn't stop thinking about him. Freddie followed her into the kitchen. She turned and faced him. "What are you doing about Max?" she demanded.

"Breaking all ties with him as soon as possible," Freddie answered, as unemotional as ever. "I'll buy him out."

"You can't do that. He's your partner," she said, reminding him of something he knew only too well.

"True. However, I have fifty-one percent, he has forty-nine. He's history."

"You might be making a mistake."

"How many times have I told you not to interfere in my business?"

"You're so insulting," she said, her face reddening. "Who was right beside you when you were building the business up? Who went out with boring movie stars and made them feel like a million dollars so they'd sign with you? I was with you every step, and don't you forget it."

"What the hell's gotten into you today?" he asked, his voice rising.

She took a gulp of coffee and let her frustration

rip. "When was the last time you touched me, Freddie?"

"Oh, God!" he groaned. "Not that again."

"You don't care, do you?"

"Of course I do."

"No, Freddie, you never liked sex much anyway, and now in the last few years . . ." She trailed off.

"Enough of this nonsense," Freddie said harshly. "I have more important matters to deal with."

Diana's anger and frustration continued to surface. "I want a man who loves me," she blurted. "In every way."

Freddie's response was completely devoid of emotion. "What are you after, a divorce?" he asked coldly.

She shook her head, frightened to tell him that yes—that's exactly what she wanted. "I . . . I don't know," she stammered.

"Pull yourself together, Diana," he said, leaving the kitchen.

She trailed him into the library. "Are you aware that Max got engaged?"

"What are you going on about now?"

"He's engaged."

"To the model who stood him up last night?"

"No, to someone called Kristin—I have no idea who she is."

"How do you know?"

"Max phoned this morning."

"Oh, did he? Abject with apology no doubt. Dying to slither back into my good graces."

"He merely told me he was engaged."

"Why didn't he announce it last night?"

"He hardly had an opportunity, the way you and Ariel ganged up on him."

"I don't intend to keep repeating myself, Diana—stay *out* of my business."

She glared at him. "If that's the way you want it. And by the way, if I *do* decide to divorce you, Freddie—how *would* you feel?"

He looked at her in astonishment that she would consider such a rash move. "Don't even think about it. We're perfectly happy. Everyone knows that."

She stomped out of the room. Freddie shook his head. What the hell was going on with her? She must be going through the change of life early. God! Poor hard-done-by Diana. Didn't she realize how lucky she was? After all, she was married to one of the most important men in town.

chapter 12

Max prowled around his house with plenty of time to spare before Kristin arrived. He didn't want to waste it doing nothing, so he called Howie to see if he was around. Howie's service picked up. Max left his name, and then decided to take a swim in his luxurious pool and maybe work on his tan for an hour or so. Might as well catch some rays, he thought, grimly acknowledging that he had nothing else to do.

Tomorrow he would face Freddie; no way was he dealing with that little problem today. He knew Freddie too well. In fact, he knew him better than anyone—which, he realized, wasn't saying a lot because nobody really knew Freddie. He was a man of mystery—impossible to bond with on a man-to-man level. He wasn't into ball games, poker, horses *or* women. Just work.

Max wandered outside, stripped off his shirt and pants and dropped into a lounge chair. He was happy in his brief white Calvins—the snug style— which emphasized his considerable assets.

As he stretched out, his mind drifted briefly to Inga Cruelle, the woman who'd stood him up last night. Supermodel bitch! She'd dumped him to go on a date with Howie Powers, whom she'd picked up at a cocktail party. How dumb could a girl get? Howie was his friend, but everyone knew the man was an idiot, a rich playboy with nothing going for him except his father's money.

Yes, Inga had really blown it. No way would he help her with her so-called movie career now; she could find herself another agent.

When he'd had enough sun, he jumped in the pool and swam, as usual overdoing it. Max never did things by halves, he always had to excel—prob- ably because when he was a kid, his father beat the crap out of him if he wasn't the best at everything he tried. After swimming, he decided he had an appetite. Lunch at The Ivy didn't seem like a bad idea; the only problem was that eating alone was not on his agenda—too loser-like.

Maybe he'd give Inga one last chance.

No, he decided. Screw her! Nobody dumped on Max Steele and got away with it.

Of course, there was a long list of other lovelies

he could call, but he wasn't in the mood to make conversation, and all most of them talked about were their careers.

Actresses. He'd had it with actresses. How nice it would be to have Kristin in his life. A natural beauty with no ambitions. And no more clients except him.

Idly he wondered how much it would cost a week to keep her. Hmm . . . she probably didn't come cheap. But what did he care? He owned half of I.A.A. and whatever happened between him and Freddie, he'd still end up with a bundle of money.

Instead of lunch he decided to go to Jhama Juice and grab a health drink. Jumping in his Maserati, he set off. The sun was shining; things weren't so bad; tomorrow he'd make everything okay with Freddie.

As he drove along San Vicente he thought about Diana Leon and how bizarre it was that she had come on to him. If Freddie ever found out, he'd choke on his own surprise.

Depending on what happened between him and Freddie, he wondered if maybe he *should* have an affair with Diana, simply to keep her on his side.

No, she was too old. He couldn't remember the last time he'd had a girl over thirty. Did they even exist in L.A.? Not in *his* mind.

He parked in the underground structure below

the health-juice bar, locked his car and began walking out of the tunnel-like structure.

"Gimme your fuckin' money, mothafucker."

Oh, Jesus! Before he could spin around he felt a gun sticking in his back. *Oh, Jesus!*

"An' take that fuckin' Rolex off, or I'll blow your mothafuckin' head off."

V

chapter 13

Van Morrison was singing "Have I Told You Lately That I Love You." As Kristin listened to the touching lyrics she felt like bursting into tears. Whenever she left Cherie, she was always in a highly emotional state. The doctor who looked in on Cherie a couple of times a week had long ago told her she should pull the plug, but she couldn't bring herself to do it. While her sister was still breathing, there was always the possibility of a miracle.

Deep down, however, she knew it wasn't realistic. Deep down she knew her precious sister already was dead.

The heartfelt lyrics enveloped her as she raced her car along the freeway. Should she tell Max about Cherie? That was the question. Maybe if he knew, he wouldn't want her. Too bad. She had a new policy—the truth above all else. If she'd been truthful with Jake she wouldn't be so miserable now.

What was Max up to anyway? She was anxious to find out. First she had to go home and change and return Darlene's call. Darlene was probably mad that she hadn't responded to last night's phone message. What did she care? She was through worrying what other people thought.

Her apartment was delightfully cool and welcoming. She'd left the air conditioning on full blast because it was one of those muggy days that L.A. denizens always said screamed earthquake weather. She'd never experienced an earthquake herself, having arrived in L.A. after the big Northridge one of '94. It seemed impossible that it could be as bad as people said, but all the same she kept a special earthquake cupboard filled with canned goods, bottled water and flashlights. If there was ever another major quake, she'd get in her car and drive straight to the nursing home. It worried her that they probably wouldn't look after Cherie properly in an emergency situation. That's why she visited every week, taking the nurses presents and candy, making sure they paid attention.

The first thing she did when she walked through the door was check her answering machine to see if Jake had called. Not that she expected him to, of course, and quite frankly, she didn't care if she ever heard from him again.

So why was her heart beating so fast as she approached her machine? Why was she willing the red message light to be flashing?

The red light *was* flashing. One flash. One message.

Probably Darlene wanting to know why she hadn't responded regarding Mister X.

She pressed down the rewind button. "Kristin," said a muffled male voice, not Jake's. "Why didn't you come last night? I do not appreciate being ignored. It is not good for either of us. Tonight. Eight. The end of Santa Monica Pier. I'll pay you double. Be there."

She was shocked. How had Mister X gotten her home number? Had Darlene given it to him? This was absolutely unacceptable.

In a fury, she picked up the phone to complain to Darlene, but Darlene's housekeeper informed her she was out. Kristin left a message for a callback and hung up, still outraged. Mister X being in possession of her home number made her feel totally vulnerable and somewhat uneasy. Having her number was only one step away from getting her address. She shivered at the thought.

Maybe Max's timing was right on target. At least if she was living with *him* she'd be protected. The more she thought about it, the more she knew it was the only sensible move.

Hurrying to her closet, she changed into a simple yellow sundress and high-heeled sandals. Then she applied some makeup and set off to close the deal with Max.

chapter 14

As he drove his truck to pick up Madison, Jake had a strong urge to call Kristin. He'd had a few drinks at his father's wedding and also time to think things over. Why *hadn't* he demanded to know what was going on? It was a puzzle he couldn't quite solve. What was Kristin doing in bed with him anyway? It wasn't like she'd asked him for money. What was her motive? And how long had she planned on keeping her profession a secret from him?

He'd seriously thought they had something together, so when he heard that woman's voice on her answering machine, he'd gone into shock. As for Kristin, she'd lain there, not saying a word in her defense. God, she must've thought he was a gullible fool.

Now he was depressed and a little bit drunk, and sorry that he'd asked Madison out to dinner. She was an attractive woman, but she wasn't Kristin. Was he supposed to stop caring about somebody simply because she turned out to be a hooker?

But how can I care for someone I don't even know? he asked himself glumly. He'd seen her three times and fallen in love. How dumb was *that?*

He parked his truck outside Natalie's house, got out and walked slowly to the front door. Jimmy had booked him a table at The Palm. "Take her there, order the steak and lobster, get her drunk, fuck her and forget about Kristin," his brother had told him.

"Is that all you think about with women? Getting laid?"

"If *you* were married to Bunny, that's all *you'd* think about. She nags me to death."

"She always did. You knew that before you married her."

"I've been meaning to tell you," Jimmy had confided. "You do know that I see other women on the side?"

Jake had no desire to listen to Jimmy's sexcapades. "What is this, confession time?" he'd said abruptly. "I don't want to hear about it."

"I'm your brother," Jimmy had said indignantly. "If I can't tell *you,* who can I tell?"

"Dad—he's the philanderer in the family. At least he marries *his* conquests."

Jake had not wanted to hear any more about his

brother's extracurricular love life. Bunny might be a pain—but it didn't seem fair that Jimmy used that as an excuse to be unfaithful.

He rang the doorbell of Natalie's house.

Cole answered. "Hey, man," he said. "How was the wedding?"

"Predictable," Jake answered, entering the small house. "My dad's sixty-two, his bride's twenty. I guess that says it all."

"You gonna call her Mommy?" Cole joked, leading him into the living room.

"I'm not going to call her, period," Jake said dryly. "I went to the wedding; I've done my duty for the year."

"You and your dad tight?"

"Is Madison around?" Jake asked, not comfortable with Cole firing questions at him.

"Yeah, I'll call her. Hey, Maddie!" Cole yelled. "Your knight in tarnished armor is here."

"Very funny," Jake said. "Can I get some water?"

"Sure." Cole left the room, returning moments later with a bottle of Evian, which he handed over.

"Thanks," Jake said, swigging from the bottle.

A few moments later Madison walked in. Jake did a slow double take. He'd known she was an attractive woman, but he hadn't realized she had such a great body and was so devastatingly beautiful. Her oval face was surrounded by a cloud of dark hair, which up until this time he'd only seen pulled back. Her seductive lips were emphasized with a brownish gold lipstick, matching the subtle shadow above her elongated eyes. She wore a red dress which took his breath away—low-cut, short, with little spaghetti straps. She looked amazing.

"Hi," she said, unaware of the effect she was having on him.

He'd gone back to his hotel after the wedding and changed out of his one and only suit into khaki pants and a denim shirt with no tie. "I feel underdressed," he said, and then he realized he had said almost the same thing to Kristin on their first date.

"Shall I go change?" Madison asked. *"I* feel half naked."

"You *look* sensational, and if you're comfortable like that . . ."

"No," she laughed, delighted to see he hadn't bothered to dress up. "I'm certainly *not*. Getting all done up was Cole and Natalie's idea. They were in a make-over mood, and I went along with them. Do you *mind* if I go change?"

"Whatever makes you happy."

She smiled. "That'll make me happy."

Two hours later they were engrossed in deep conversation. Madison had put on a loose sweater, black jeans and a casual jacket. But she had left her hair down and not removed her makeup. Men's heads turned. She was a striking woman.

Jake found her fascinating because he could talk to her in a way he couldn't talk to most women. She was sharp and savvy and knew everything that was going on, yet she wasn't a know-it-all. She listened intently to what he had to say and had a throaty laugh he found quite enticing. They'd already discussed politics, religion, the state of the movie industry, publishing, pornography on the Internet and his favorite subject—photography. Madison was a stimulating conversationalist.

"Where are you from originally?" he asked, taking a bite of one of the best steaks he'd ever tasted.

"I'm a true New Yorker," she said. "In fact, my parents still live there. Well actually, they don't— they moved to Connecticut."

"What does your dad do?"

She was silent for a moment. "Uh . . . he's in commodities."

"Commodities," Jake said. "The stock market?"

"Kind of."

"I don't get the stock market," Jake said. "It's like legalized gambling to me."

"Have you ever been to Vegas?"

"Haven't been. Don't want to go."

"Damn!" Madison said with a low sexy laugh. "There goes my plan of taking you there for a long weekend of unbridled lust."

Jake sat up very straight. "Huh?"

"Just joking," she said with a tantalizing smile.

He was confused; under virtually any other circumstances he would have found this woman completely irresistible. But he had to be honest with himself and admit that his mind was still on

Kristin. All night he kept on wondering what she was doing and if she was thinking about him.

"Why don't you tell me about her," Madison said, leaning forward, her eyes bright with genuine interest. "I'm an excellent listener. In fact, it's part of my job."

"Tell you about whom?"

"Listen," she said, matter-of-factly. "Three months ago I broke up with my boyfriend. Or rather *he* broke up with *me*. Now believe me, I *know* it takes time to get over something like that. I'm almost there; you're obviously just starting."

He considered denying it, then thought—why not be honest? She was too smart and too nice to try and fake it. So he began telling her his story, while she listened attentively—interjecting an occasional wise comment.

"That's it," he said when he'd finished his sorry tale. "And like an idiot, I told my asshole brother, who announced it to everyone at our dad's wedding. Now I feel like the world's biggest jerk."

"Don't," she said, shaking her head. "Your reaction was perfectly understandable. You felt out of control and betrayed."

"That's exactly it!" he said excitedly. "Hey— were you ever a shrink?"

"No—but I write stories, so I know people. My father taught me how to analyze situations and sum up the players. He's a brilliant man."

"So . . . what's my next move?"

"You call her up, apologize for bolting like a

frightened rabbit and make a date for lunch on neutral territory."

"Are you sure?"

"Yes. You have to give her a chance to explain why she didn't tell you."

"Good," he said, relieved. "I can't wait to hear what she has to say."

"Remember," Madison said sternly. "No accusations. Simply hear her out."

"I'll do it," he said, finishing off his steak.

"You won't be sorry," she said, taking a quick peek at her watch. "Now, do you mind if we leave? I want to catch the ten o'clock news, see if there's anything new on Salli's murder."

"No problem," he said, calling for the check. Then he looked at her long and hard. "Y'know, if this was another time, another place—"

"I know," she said softly. "You don't have to say a word. We'll get together again when we're both feeling a little less vulnerable. How's that?"

He grinned. "You're a great lady."

She grinned back. "And you're a great guy. So let's get the hell out of here!"

chapter 15

Since Captain Marsh was demanding an arrest in the murder of Salli T. Turner within twenty-four hours, Detective Tucci knew that he had to put the rest of the day to good use. The fact that Bobby Skorch had summoned his lawyer and refused to talk to them had aroused Tucci's suspicions. If Bobby had nothing to hide, then why wouldn't he allow himself to be questioned? he wondered. And why wasn't he anxious to find out the details of his wife's brutal murder?

After their meeting with Captain Marsh, Lee decided he should get on the next plane to Vegas so he could thoroughly check up on Bobby Skorch's every move from the previous day.

While Lee was taking care of things in Vegas,

Tucci interviewed Eddie Stoner, Salli's ex. The good news was that Eddie's lawyer had not arrived to bail him out. The bad news was that Eddie was in a vile mood.

"What the fuck am I bein' held for?" Eddie demanded, wild bloodshot eyes bulging with fury as he sat at the interview table.

"Parking tickets," Tucci said, pulling up a chair. "Too many of 'em."

"So where the *fuck* is my lawyer?"

"You had your phone call, Eddie."

"Well," Eddie said truculently. "I want another goddamn phone call."

"You know the rules—one call."

"This is a joke," Eddie snarled. "I'm tellin' my fuckin' union 'bout this shit."

"What union?"

"The Screen Actors Guild, that's who. No way they'll let their members be treated like this."

"Where were you last night, Eddie?"

"I want a lawyer present before I answer any questions."

"Why? You got something to hide?"

"I need a cigarette."

"Sure, Eddie. Let me get you one."

Tucci got up and left the room. He could see that Eddie Stoner was a nervous wreck, and it wasn't just for the want of a cigarette—he was obviously hooked on something stronger than nicotine, and he was starting to miss it badly.

Tucci bummed a cigarette from the desk sergeant and reentered the interview room. "Here you go."

"Thanks," Eddie said, grabbing the cigarette and lighting up.

Tucci took a moment to study him. Eddie was good-looking in a dissolute way. Although only thirty, he had bags under his eyes that you could take on a trip, a long mane of dirty blond hair, flat blue eyes and a mean scowl. He was wearing an old Nike T-shirt, jeans that had seen better days and scuffed sneakers.

"I'd like to see you go home today," Tucci said. "So let's make this easy on everybody and you tell me where you were last night."

"Let me ask you somethin'," Eddie said, dragging hungrily on his cigarette. "What's so important about where I was last night? You hauled me in on parking tickets, not a fuckin' murder."

Tucci studied him. From that remark, it would appear that he didn't know about Salli T. Turner's murder. Or maybe he was playing it smart. "What's preventing you from answering?" the detective asked.

"'Cause I don't 'preciate bein' dragged outta bed in the middle of the night. You guys have fuckin' balls of steel."

"Just doing our job."

"Yeah, well, when I do *my* fuckin' job, I don't hassle people in the middle of the night."

"Y'know," Tucci said. "Unrelated to this little mess, you're a very good actor. I've seen you in a couple of movies. Shame you never got that big break."

"You bet your ass it's a shame," Eddie said excitedly. "I look at the assholes who make it an' I gotta say to myself—why the *hell* isn't it me? Jean-Claude Van Damme: what the fuck's *he* got that I haven't? I'm better lookin', an' I'm *certainly* a better actor."

"Right, Eddie," Tucci agreed. "You're also an American."

"You bet your ass."

"So, I'll tell you what I'll do, Eddie. Since your lawyer hasn't responded, I'll let you make another call if you tell me where you were last night."

Eddie ran a hand through his long hair. "Let me think," he said. "I picked up a coupla chicks at a club on Sunset. Went back to their place 'round midnight, got crazy outta my skull. I musta got home around three."

"Who were the girls?"

Eddie laughed dryly. "You think I ask their names?"

"You mean you spent the night with two women, and you don't know who they are?" Tucci asked, knowing he must sound like some out-of-touch old fogy.

"This is Hollywood, man—chicks are everywhere. Who gives a shit what they're called?"

"Try to remember, Eddie."

"Hey—you're not *listenin'* to me," Eddie said irritably. "I dunno who they were. Picked 'em up in a club. *They* were horny—*I* was horny. We all got off."

"Do you remember what club it was?"

"I was in the Viper Room earlier. Maybe it was a place called The Boss."

"Does The Boss have a doorman?"

"They got a bouncer."

"Would he know who the girls are?"

"Hey, man, he's not lookin' to identify no one. All he's lookin' for is a big, fat tip."

"Okay, Eddie."

"Do I get my call?"

"Yes. Only I don't want you leaving town. Oh, and by the way—"

"What?"

"Your ex-wife—"

"Salli?"

"She was murdered last night."

"Oh, *fuck!*" Eddie said, his upper body slumping onto the table. "Oh, fuck! Now you're gonna tell me you think I have somethin' t'do with it?"

"I'm not saying anything," Tucci said. "But don't leave the city. Is that clear?"

"How'd it happen?" Eddie asked, sitting up. "Was it that moron she married? I warned her he was trouble."

"When did you last see her?" Tucci asked.

"Hey, man," Eddie said, throwing up his hands. "I may *look* stupid—but I know when it's time for no more questions. I need a lawyer."

Tucci got up and headed for the door, where he stopped for a brief moment studying Eddie's expression. "She was stabbed to death," he said. "Multiple times. I'll make sure you get your phone call."

chapter 16

As she drove to Max's house in Bel Air, Kristin made another attempt to listen to the Bob Evans biography on tape. Once again she couldn't concentrate and turned it off. She tried to steer her thoughts away from Jake, thinking instead of Cherie and the nursing home. Her sister had looked paler than usual today. The doctor who took care of her had left a message with one of the nurses that he wished to speak with her. Since Dr. Raine was never at the nursing home on Sundays, her only real day off, she knew she had to call him, but she kept putting it off; whatever he had to say she was certain it would not be good. Dr. Raine was a nice man, but he didn't understand about miracles.

She often thought about the day she and Cherie

had gotten in their battered old car and set off for Los Angeles. Cherie had been so excited, in fact, it was she who had instigated the trip. "We're going to be famous actresses," Cherie had promised, her pretty face glowing with anticipation. "Both of us. And we'll *never* be jealous of each other. We'll *never* have any of that stupid sibling rivalry."

Three months after they left home, their parents were killed in a train wreck, so there was no going back. The tragedy had drawn them even closer, since they then had no one except each other—at least until Howie Powers entered their lives, a man Kristin hated with a burning intensity. She'd neither seen nor heard from him since the accident. He obviously couldn't have cared less whether Cherie lived or died.

Kristin wondered what Cherie would think of what she was doing now to make a living. There was no doubt that her sister would disapprove, but what choice did she have? The nursing home bills had to be paid, and she couldn't make a living as an actress—too tough a profession by far. Besides, she'd never studied, nor ever had any ambition in that direction. Cherie had been the ambitious one. Cherie had envisioned stardom for both of them.

The gates to Max's house were closed. Strange how in the affluent neighborhoods of L.A. everyone surrounded themselves with iron gates, guard dogs and elaborate alarm systems, Kristin thought.

They lived in fortresses. Who did they expect was coming to get them?

She got out of her car and rang the outside buzzer. No reply. She rang it again, then glanced at her watch. It was almost five o'clock, and she'd told him she would be here at four. Had he not bothered to wait?

She rang again and again. Nothing.

After ten minutes of trying she realized nobody was home. Had Max Steele changed his mind? Was that it? He'd invited a hooker to move in, and then he'd reconsidered.

Angrily she got back into her car. Why was it that every man she met let her down? How come they were all a bunch of selfish, sex-crazed, perverted bastards?

Then it occurred to her. If she was going to deal with bastards, she may as well get paid for it.

Mister X's words ran through her head. *I'll pay you double.*

Double was good. In Mister X's case, double meant a great deal of money.

Who needs you, Max Steele? You couldn't even leave a note for me. Whatever happened to common courtesy?

Backing her car out of the driveway and into the winding street, she drove home.

When the bullet hit Max it was like a sharp blinding jolt from hell. He felt as if his shoulder was being torn away from his body, and he screamed out in pure agony. This wasn't a movie. This was the real thing. And he could not believe it was happening to him.

He had given the bastard his Rolex, much as he hated doing so. He had handed over his money as well—all twenty bucks of it—which was every dollar he had on him.

The meager sum clearly had made the guy mad. "You're drivin' a freakin' Maserati," the robber snarled, ski mask concealing his face. "A cocksuckin' Maserati, an' you're walkin' around with twenty pissin' bucks. Don't jack me off, mothafucker."

"That's all I have," Max had responded with a shrug.

"Fuck you, you rich bastard!" the robber screamed. And then he had fired a shot—just like that.

Max fell to the ground. The robber didn't seem to care whether he died or not. He kicked him in the groin with the sharp tip of his cowboy boot before he grabbed the keys of the Maserati and drove off, leaving Max lying there in a pool of blood.

He lost consciousness almost immediately, until somewhere in the distance he heard a child's voice yelling, "Mommy! Mommy! There's a man lying down. Mommy! Mommy!"

And the worried mother's voice answering, "Don't look, darling. Stay away from him. Get in the car and lock your door."

Oh Jesus! What did they think he was—some falling down drunk bum? He tried to speak, his voice weak as he managed to croak, "Somebody . . . gotta help me."

The woman said, "You should be ashamed of yourself!" Then she must have noticed the ever widening pool of blood, because she suddenly gasped, "Oh, my God! You've been shot!"

"Get . . . the . . . police . . . ," he mumbled. "Go for help. . . ." And he slumped back, wondering if he was dying.

The woman jumped in her car and phoned the police on her cell phone. She even waited until they arrived.

The next thing Max remembered was lying in an ambulance as it raced him to an emergency room, sirens screaming.

He couldn't believe it. He, Max Steele, had gotten himself shot.

Then everything went black.

chapter 17

Lucinda's call caught Freddie by surprise. He was in his study, contemplating Diana's foul mood and Max's unconscionable behavior when she phoned. "Darling," she drawled, as only a superstar of Lucinda's caliber could. "I desperately need a favor."

"What?" he asked, suspicious as always of movie stars courting favors.

Manhattan Style is doing a cover story on me," she informed him. "The editor, Victor Simons, is an old friend, so I know it'll be a positive piece. However, Victor has asked me to do him a personal favor which involves you." A dramatic pause. "Darling, the magazine wants to profile *you.*"

"Lucinda, you know I don't do publicity," he said, keeping his voice pleasant and even.

"Yes, Freddie, darling, I do know that. But if you did this for me, they'd give you full copy approval, so what's to lose?"

"My privacy," he said grimly.

"*What* privacy?" she retorted, as if it was the most amusing thing she'd ever heard. "You're acknowledged to be the most famous agent in Hollywood. You *should* do it, Freddie. After all, Sumner Redstone is in all the media; so is Michael Eisner."

"Sumner owns the world, Michael runs a studio," Freddie pointed out.

"Who knows," Lucinda said. "Perhaps that's what *you'll* do one of these days."

"Mike Ovitz already made that mistake," he said, annoyed because he knew he was going to have to say yes. Recently he'd persuaded Lucinda to sign for a movie she really didn't want to do. It was a twelve-million-dollar deal—which meant almost a two-million-dollar commission for the agency. How *could* he turn her down?

"Well, anyway," Lucinda said, bored with the conversation. "I *would* like to tell Victor yes, that you'll meet his reporter tomorrow at eleven. Can you accommodate me, Freddie—please? I hardly *ever* ask favors. Please?"

"What's the name of the reporter?" he asked resignedly.

"Madison something or other. Apparently she's very good."

"Is she aware I get copy approval?"

"It doesn't matter whether she knows or not. Victor Simons is the editor."

"Only for you, Lucinda," Freddie said, sighing. "Have Victor send me a fax confirming I have copy *and* headline approval."

"Thank you, darling," she cooed. "I knew you wouldn't let me down."

When she hung up, it occurred to him that the woman she'd mentioned must be the same journalist Ria had told him about. That's all he needed—an interview with some nosy journalist prying into his life.

The phone rang again. "Yes?" he said impatiently.

"Mr. Leon?"

"Who's this?"

"I'm phoning from Cedar Sinai."

Freddie felt his stomach turn. Why was he getting a phone call from a hospital? "What is it?"

"Max Steele was recently admitted. We thought you should be informed immediately."

"Admitted for what?"

"Mr. Steele was shot during a robbery."

Freddie was silent. He didn't know how to digest this piece of information; it seemed so unreal. "How bad is he?" he asked at last.

"It's critical. We have him in intensive care."

"I'll be right there," Freddie said, slamming the phone down and jumping up from his desk. "Diana!" he yelled. "Diana!"

She was sitting in the living room reading a book

on Oriental art, studiously pretending to ignore him.

"You won't believe this one," he said. "We have to get over to Cedar's immediately. Max has been shot."

Diana leaped out of her chair. "What!" she exclaimed, the color draining from her face. "How? Where?"

"Apparently it was a robbery."

"How serious is it?" she asked.

"I don't know. Let's go."

"Oh, my God!" she said, her face crumpling. "Oh, my God!" And suddenly she burst into tears.

"Pull yourself together," Freddie said tersely. "Hysterics aren't going to help anyone."

And even though he was mad at Max and felt he'd been betrayed, Freddie was panicked at the thought of anything happening to him.

chapter 18

"**H**ow was it?" Cole asked the moment Madison walked in.

"What are *you* doing here?" she said, surprised to see him. "I thought you had a hot date."

"Got canceled," he answered.

"That must've pleased Natalie," she said, shrugging off her jacket.

"You could say she's thrilled. There's no way she approves of me seein' Mr. Mogul." He indicated his dinner laid out on the coffee table. Pizza, a carton of French fries and a large-size Diet Coke. "Hey—wanna piece of pizza?"

"What happened to your health foods?"

He grinned, patting his finely muscled stomach. "Sometimes you gotta give it up."

She settled on the couch. "What was his reason for canceling?" she asked, stealing a French fry.

Cole made a "how would I know" gesture. "Dunno. Don't care," he said vaguely.

She could see he was hurt. "I'm sure it was a good one."

"Who knows," he said, picking up another piece of pizza. "Oh, by the way, some dude called Victor wants you to call him."

"My editor," she said, reaching for the phone and waking Victor up in New York—which seemed to be becoming a habit. "What's going on, Victor?" she asked.

"You have your interview with Freddie Leon," he said, sounding pleased with himself. "Tomorrow, eleven o'clock, his office. *Be* there!"

"I'm impressed," she said, delighted that he'd finally delivered on his promise. "How did you arrange it?"

"Let's just say my connection came through."

"How long will he give me?"

"Use your charm, Madison. I'm sure you'll get as long as you want."

"Thanks, Victor—I love it when you deliver."

"Good news?" Cole asked when she hung up the phone.

"Excellent," Madison said. "I've got my interview with the elusive Mr. Leon."

"So, c'mon," Cole said. "Tell me all about your date."

"Actually, it was very nice," she said, curling her

legs under her. "Jake's a terrific guy. He's also completely enamored with someone else, but that doesn't make him a bad guy. We had a great time, talked about everything. Then I gave him advice on his love life. How's that?"

"Doesn't sound too romantic to me."

"It's not supposed to," she said. "Can we switch channels and watch the news? I'd like to see if there's any new developments in the Salli T. Turner murder."

"They identified the blonde those two surfers pulled out the ocean today."

"They did? Who is she?"

"Some girl from Idaho."

"Really?"

"What they're saying is she was drowned in a swimming pool, *then* dumped in the ocean. How about *that?*"

"God, there's some sickos out there," Madison said, shivering. "Anything new on Salli?"

"The same old crap. One moment she's the Virgin Mary, the next she's the biggest slut who ever walked, depending on what channel you're watching."

Madison really wanted to get into bed and watch TV there, but she had a strong suspicion Cole felt like having company. "Is Natalie back?" she asked.

"If I know my sister, she will *not* be comin' home tonight," Cole said with a big grin. "I took a look at Luther when he came to pick her up. Boy, he's a big one."

"Yeah—just the way Natalie likes 'em."

They both giggled. "Hey, Maddie," Cole said. "It's cool you had a good time."

"Jake's an interesting man," she said. "However, I can promise you this—I am *not* in the frame of mind to get involved with anybody right now. And since he's already involved, no problem."

"Not into one-nighters, huh?" Cole said teasingly.

"No," she answered firmly. "And you shouldn't be either—too dangerous."

"I often wonder what it must've been like in the sixties—when sex wasn't gonna get you zapped. When you could do anything and not have to pay with your life."

"Yeah," she said. "It must have been pretty nice then. That's when my mom and dad got together."

"You talk about your dad a lot. You're real tight with him, huh?"

"I certainly am. He's a wonderful man."

"And your mom?"

"She's great, too, but I've always been closer to Michael. He taught me how to get out in the world and go after what I wanted. He taught me to be fair, and, most of all, he taught me to follow my dreams."

"Michael sounds like quite a guy."

"He is."

Luther was a romantic. He took Natalie to a small restaurant in Santa Monica overlooking the ocean. It happened to be located in the hotel he was staying at—Shutters on the Beach. Of course, he omitted to tell her this vital piece of information as he plied her with red wine and compliments.

"Y'know, baby," he crooned in a low-down, smoky voice. "I feel like you an' I—well—like we was an accident waitin' to happen."

Natalie leaned across the table. It wasn't exactly how she would've put it, but he had a point. And she was quite ready to jump into bed with him and start what she was sure would be a more-than-satisfying sexual relationship. Even though Luther lived in Chicago, he could visit on a regular basis, and that would make seeing him all the more exciting.

He reached for her hand, pressing his strong fingers up against hers. She felt the heat and smiled to herself. Oh, baby, this was going to be finger-licking good!

And then her cell phone went off. "Damn!" she exclaimed, scrambling in her purse to answer the stupid thing. It was Garth, her station manager.

"We need you here immediately," Garth said tersely. "We got a lead on the Malibu blonde. Turns out she might be part of a high-priced call girl ring. I want you to come in right now and put together a story on her."

"Now?" Natalie objected. "I'm in the middle of a date."

"You can get laid anytime," Garth said rudely. "This is important."

"How important?"

"You're always whining that you want to get into real news. If you do a good job, this could be the start of a whole other direction for you."

"News anchor?" she questioned breathlessly.

"Don't get carried away."

"I'll be there," she said, clicking off her phone. Suddenly Luther's luster dimmed. He was big and sexy, but he was, after all, only a guy. "Uh . . . Luther," she said.

"Yeah, baby?"

"I know you're a real understanding guy, so if I told you I had to go to work . . . could we pick this up where we left off—say tomorrow night?"

"But baby—"

"I know, I know," she said softly. "It's a real bummer, an' I'll miss you like crazy—"

He shook his head like he couldn't quite believe this was happening to him. He was a man *definitely* not used to a woman putting work before him.

"Go with me on this, Luther," she murmured sweetly. "And I promise, tomorrow we'll make it a night to remember."

Before he could object, she was on her feet and out the door.

chapter 19

Angela Musconni, the hot nine-teen-year-old movie star with a bad drug habit, was in bed with her current boyfriend, Kevin Page, another hot young movie star, with *no* bad drug habit, when the phone rang.

They'd been in bed all day as they'd partied all night and not gotten to sleep until five in the morning.

Angie stretched out a long naked arm, wearily groping for the receiver. "Yes," she mumbled. "Who's wakin' me up?"

"Angelina," said a voice, echoing from her past.

"Who's this?" she asked suspiciously, although a familiar gnawing in the pit of her stomach told her exactly who it was.

"You know I'm the only one who calls you Angelina."

"Eddie?" she questioned sharply. "Is that you?"

"Yep, it's the man himself."

"Wadda *you* want?"

"I want you to bail me outta jail."

"What *are* you talking about?" she said, struggling to sit up.

"I'm in deep shit, Angie. Can't reach my lawyer, an' I dunno who else to call who'd have the money to bail me. I gotta get outta here *now*. The cops told me Salli's bin murdered, an' they got their eye on me."

"I haven't spoken to you in three freakin' years," she said accusingly, finally becoming fully alert. "Ever since you ran out on me and married Salli."

"I know, babe, but if old friendships mean anythin', you gotta come and get me. I can't take it here."

"Jeez!" Angie said, completely amazed that he had the nerve to call her. "Is *that* why they've arrested you? *Did* you do it, you bastard?"

"No fuckin' way," he said indignantly. "I'm here 'cause of some crap about unpaid parking tickets."

"You were always threatening us, Eddie," she said, remembering the past. "Me *and* her."

Kevin rolled over in his sleep. "Whoissit?"

"Nobody."

"You gonna come?" Eddie demanded.

"Why should I?"

"Oh Christ! I need you, Angelina."

Angie was torn; on one hand she was outraged that after all this time Eddie had called her, and on the other her natural curiosity was fast getting the better of her. "Maybe," she said grudgingly.

"What does 'maybe' mean?" Eddie blustered. "You comin' or not?"

"I'll see," she said, putting the phone down and breaking the connection. She stared at Kevin, who didn't stir. Carefully she edged her way out of bed.

Kevin grabbed her bare leg, startling her. "Where you goin'," he mumbled.

"I gotta go out," she said briskly. "Emergency."

"Bring food," he said, as he rolled over and promptly went back to sleep.

She ran to the bathroom and pulled on a pair of tight jeans and a midriff-baring sweater. She knew Kevin always kept a stack of bills stashed beneath his pile of T-shirts, so she went to his dresser drawer and helped herself to a bundle.

Why am I doing this? she asked herself. *Sure, I loved Eddie once, but the asshole dumped on me big time. Now he's probably hacked up Salli, and I'm the one springing him from jail. What's* wrong *with me?*

But Angie always *had* gotten off on excitement, and this was the most exciting thing to have happened to her in a long time. Being a movie star was way too safe and predictable. Living on the edge—that's the way she liked it.

And there was nobody better than Eddie Stoner for taking you on a trip to the wild side, and then right to the very edge.

chapter 20

From her chic, upswept, dark blond hair, to the tips of her finely manicured, blood red, inch-long nails, Darlene La Porte was one of the best-groomed women in Beverly Hills. It took a lot of money to look like Darlene—plenty of big bucks, considering she kept a team of professionals always on call to attend to her grooming needs. She had a hairdresser who came to her house every morning. Then there was her manicurist, dietician, makeup artist, clothes stylist, yoga instructor and personal trainer. They were all on Darlene's payroll. She was no movie star, but she took better care of herself than most of them did.

The payoff was worth it. She looked thirty. She was actually forty-one.

A youthful appearance was extremely important

to Darlene. She needed to interact and relate to the young girls who worked for her. Every month there was a new batch of pretty girls who arrived in Hollywood hoping to become actresses or models. When their dreams faded—which invariably happened fast—Darlene was there to lead them on to another path. She offered them glamour and excitement and big money. She offered them movie stars and moguls and intimacy with all the men they'd have no chance of getting anywhere near in real life. Once they were thoroughly initiated, she then had them service the rest of her client list—those men with unspoken demands and demented perversions. Men such as Mister X.

Darlene had no idea who Mister X was. She only knew that he grossly overpaid, and that was enough to keep her perfectly happy. The only interaction she'd ever had with him was over the phone. Last night he had called to book a repeat performance with Kristin. When he phoned back an hour later, she had to tell him that she had been unable to reach Kristin. He'd sounded angry. She had asked him if he wanted another girl. He said no. Then five minutes later he called back again and said yes—but only if she had someone fresh and new. Darlene immediately thought of Hildie, a pretty blonde from the Midwest who'd only been a working girl for two months. She and Mister X had arranged a meeting place, and Darlene had called to tell Hildie. "This guy's a tiny bit weird," she'd warned her, thinking of Kristin's complaints. "But he's not dangerous, and here's the good news—he pays *really big!*"

"Sounds like fun!" Hildie had said with all the confidence of youth.

Now Darlene sat in front of her television staring at a picture of Hildie on the news, taken at her high school prom. Hildie at sixteen with braces on her teeth and brown frizzy hair. Hardly the same girl Darlene had sent out on a date with death. The Hildie that she knew was blond and sleek. Hollywood and four years of experience had given her a totally new image.

Now she was dead.

Drowned.

Not in the ocean where she was found. In a swimming pool.

And Darlene remembered another of her girls who'd ended up fished out of the ocean. A year ago. Kimberly. By the time Kimberly's body was discovered, there was not much left to identify.

Three weeks prior to her body washing up on the beach, Kimberly also had gone on a date with Mister X.

Darlene had chosen not to connect the two events. Kimberly had been a wild party girl—into coke and heroin. Darlene imagined that she'd died under unfortunate circumstances—maybe partying with friends after her appointment with Mister X. Darlene had not called the police.

Now Hildie.

And Darlene knew that if she went to the police

this time the publicity would be so overwhelming that in no time she would become public property like Heidi Fleiss. After that, her lucrative call girl business would be over.

There was only one way to deal with such a terrible event. Never send any of her girls out with Mister X again.

Yes, she decided, even though it meant giving up a healthy amount of commission, that's exactly what she would do.

Conscience assuaged, she began switching channels until she found an old Ava Gardner movie.

Ah . . . she thought. Whatever happened to Hollywood glamour?

Darlene settled comfortably into her couch, and within minutes was totally engrossed in the movie.

chapter 21

Since Mister X had not stipulated that she wear any particular outfit or color, Kristin chose to go with scarlet. She felt bold and bad and vengeful—while deep inside she felt hurt and abandoned and useless.

Jake didn't want her.

Even Max Steele had rejected her.

And Cherie lay in the nursing home—never showing any improvement—simply lying there, wasting away—waiting for her to pull the plug.

Once in a while Kristin did a little cocaine to take away the pain. Tonight she indulged, snorting the insidious white powder, all the while hating herself for doing so. And yet she knew it would make her feel better, set her up for her date with Mister X. After all, he deserved the best, didn't he?

Because her mystery man was the only one who seemed to care about her.

Two sharp, final snorts and she was done.

Every time she did cocaine she vowed it would be the last. Yet, when her supply ran out, she'd always call Darlene and set up another delivery.

She stared at her reflection in the mirror. *Kristin. Call girl supreme. Worthless whore.*

The scarlet dress looked sensational on her. Her blond hair swirled around her fresh gorgeous face.

She took a deep breath, grabbed her purse and left her apartment.

Mister X . . . here I come. . . .

And I promise—you will not be disappointed.

TO BE CONTINUED . . .

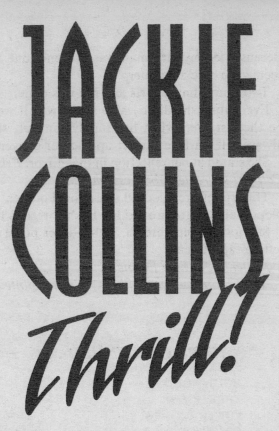

JACKIE COLLINS

Thrill!

AMERICA'S MOST SENSATIONAL NOVELIST

Available now in paperback from Pocket Books

POCKET
BOOKS

1488-02